RECOVERY

ii

RECOVERY

A Grayson Cooper Adventure

Outer Banks Series – Episode 1

by Douglas Brisotti

ISBN: 9781706705284
Printed in the USA

First printing edition 2019.

Published by:
Next Chapter Holdings, LLC
3741 Greene's Crossing
Greensboro, NC 27410

For Sarah, Kira and Ella.

You inspire me to be better every day.

North Carolina's Outer Banks

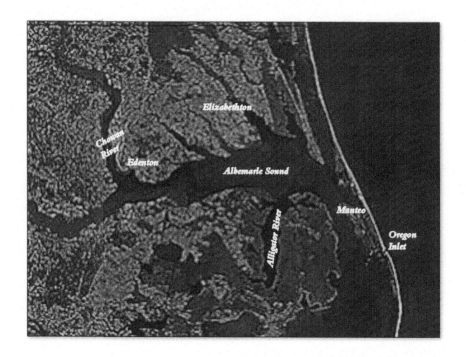

Table of Contents

Chapter 1 1

Chapter 2 8

Chapter 3 14

Chapter 4 21

Chapter 5 29

Chapter 6 34

Chapter 7 42

Chapter 8 47

Chapter 9 56

Chapter 10 64

Chapter 11 70

Chapter 12 78

Chapter 13 84

Chapter 14 94

Chapter 15 100

Chapter 16 109

Chapter 17 114

Chapter 18 120

Chapter 19 122

Chapter 20 127

Epilogue 132

Common Boating Terms

Bow – the front of the boat

Stern – the rear of the boat

Port – the left side of the boat

Starboard – the right side of the boat

Forward – moving towards the front end of the boat

Aft – moving towards the rear end of the boat

Underway – when the boat is moving

Ahead – when the boat is moving in a forward direction

Astern – when the boat is moving in a backwards direction

Amidships or Midship – the central part of the boat

Topside – moving to the upper deck of the boat

Below – moving to the below deck or cabin of the boat

Salon – the main living area on a boat; the living room

Galley – the kitchen on a boat

Head – the bathroom on a boat

Chapter 1

Sea water is blasting high into the air as the bow of the 36-foot Blackfin Sportfish crashes down off the top of a six-foot swell. A strong wind gusting to 35 knots is pushing the bay out toward the ocean directly into an incoming tide, slowing the flow and creating steep waves in the vessel's path. Oregon Inlet can be a challenge on even a mild weather day due to its currents and varying sea floor; add these conditions and a moonless night and the task of moving from bay to ocean is proving a great challenge to both vessel and crew.

The Blackfin is a well-built fishing vessel, heavy in fiberglass construction and with enough power to maneuver when needed. Each time the boat falls from the top of one wave, its nose nearly submerging into the next, the Captain increases power to the diesel powerplants and drives up the next wave before pulling back on the throttles to surf down the other side. The knuckles of his left hand white with the force of his grip on the steering wheel, Miguel periodically looks back at the rolled swim mat resting against the back of the cockpit. Its bright green color looks oddly cheery in this violent environment.

While the Blackfin and Captain are working together to reach the Atlantic, the first mate is simply holding on for dear life. Hector's left hand is clinging tightly to a rail installed for exactly this purpose mounted to the cabin wall in front of him, his right hand alternating between the top of the windscreen and signing himself. His lips move in mostly silent prayer with the occasional swear word mixed in.

Miguel looks over to Hector. "You secured that mat, no?" he says speaking loudly to be heard over the wind, waves and engine noise.

"S-s-s-si," Hector stammers, reaching again for the windscreen and gripping it tightly as the boat crests another wave. As the boat hits the bottom of the trough on the other side, Hector takes advantage of the control the motor gives while climbing and throws up over the port side. Reaching the top, he grabs the windscreen again as the boat crests and begins its plunge down the other side.

Miguel is thinking back to all the things that went wrong making this trip a necessity. *If José could have just kept his mouth shut, none of this would have happened!* None of them like the men they work for but fighting back has never resulted in anything good. He peers back at the swim mat again, this time picturing his friend, dead inside of it. Miguel says a quick prayer.

Miguel pauses a little too long with his eyes astern instead of forward. He feels the boat beginning to crest the wave and turns his head forward again, astonished at what he sees. On the shallows on either side of the inlet, all hell is breaking loose. Waves are crashing over the sandbars that move constantly off the coast of North Carolina's Outer Banks. Even worse, it is difficult to discern the channel from the bars except with the GPS. The white foam created by breaking waves all around him looks angry, and there is no obvious direction to take evasive action.

"Hold on!" he unnecessarily shouts to Hector who in the last twenty minutes hasn't let go of anything other than the contents of his stomach. The boat hits the bottom of the wave it has just crested, torpedoing into the next wave, water rushing over the top of the bow. The wave is split by the windscreen as the bow pops up and out of the water once again. The Blackfin launches off the top of the next wave, flying for a moment before crashing down at the bottom again.

This time, the wave in front of them is already breaking. The top of the wave lands in the center of the bow and the vessel submarines through it like a surfer diving for his life. The Blackfin is a rugged competitor and comes out the other side of the wave launching seawater high into the air, half the vessel airborne again as it falls to the bottom with a hull-shuttering boom.

Miguel is throttling up into the next wave trying to beat the timing of the break but doesn't make it. Once again, the boat is almost covered by the ocean, and once again, the sturdy Blackfin comes out the other side, upright and running.

Finally, they clear the sandbar and the seas become relatively calm; only three to four feet now. Miguel looks down at his hands and realizes he is still gripping the wheel for dear life. As he loosens his hands, he looks over at Hector who is gripping the windshield and vomiting over the side.

"You are going to have to clean that up, amigo," Miguel tells him, a smirk on his face.

"Fuck you," Hector replies in perfect English.

Laughing, Miguel turns stern to check his wake. "Dios Mio!!" he exclaims as he sees the mat unrolled, still tied on and dragging behind the boat. "Take the wheel Hector!" he yells as he jumps down from the flybridge helm into the cockpit. A quick inspection of the small space and of the swim platform and his fears are confirmed; the body is gone.

6

"Shit, shit, shit, shit..." Hector keeps saying over and over. While his English pronunciation isn't great most of the time, swear words seem to come naturally to him.

"Shit is right my friend," Miguel agrees as he climbs the ladder up to the flybridge and takes the helm back from Hector.

Miguel begins to slowly bring the boat around toward shore back the way they came. He turns on the spotlight and scans the waves and the sandbars, hoping to see something that will indicate where his friend's body has gone. He doesn't dare go back into the waves, but instead moves parallel with the shore, back and forth scanning the white foam.

After more than thirty minutes of this, it is clear that the body is gone.

"You will say NOTHING about this Hector, NOTHING! Do you understand?"

"S-s-s-si."

"We will go back now. Keep an eye out and use the spotlight if you need to. Let me know if you see anything!"

With the wind in their face now, the tide pushing them in, the Blackfin surfs down waves throwing water high into the air as they hit the bottom, almost all of it flying back into their faces. Not surprisingly, they find nothing.

Miguel and Hector return to port soaking wet and frightened of the consequences if Jefe ever finds out what happened tonight.

Chapter 2

I pull back on the throttles, the Whaler coming down off plane, the bow resting gently back onto the light chop of the Albemarle Sound. I idle toward my target keeping it to starboard, shifting into reverse for a few seconds before putting the throttles back into neutral the boat stopping, "Dead in the water."

"That's horrible dude," Scott Parker says as he leans his long, lean frame over the starboard side of the boat, reaching out toward our objective. Apparently, I said that last part out loud. I tend to do that. I am always commentating on my life inside of my head even as I am living it, like I am watching myself from a broadcast booth. I started doing this a long ago when things were easier, yet harder at the same time. I guess doing play-by-play and color commentary on parts of my life has provided some escape.

I am Grayson Cooper, Captain of an inland bay and nearshore private marine patrol boat on North Carolina's Outer Banks. Most people just call me "Coop." I work as a contractor to the Dare County Sheriff's Office assisting with marine-related incidents. Scott is my first mate, a former rescue swimmer with the Coast Guard who looks the part perfectly. He is six foot three and weighs just under 200 pounds. His wingspan is wider than he is tall, and he has large hands, long legs and flipper-like feet. His muscle-mass is lean and pronounced, even now in his mid-thirties. He has dark blonde hair lightened a bit by the sun, wavy with bangs that often fall into his face when not being blown back by a sea breeze, or slicked back by sea water. In a lot of ways, he resembles Michael Phelps, but without the gold medals and the weed.

Scott joined me about two years ago and is much of the expertise that led to our specialty. While we are called on to remove flotsam from the waterways to avoid recreational and commercial vessel damage, we regularly find ourselves like we are today, recovering the dead from the sea. The waters that flow around our islands, crash on our beaches and pull on our sandy shores all too often take human life with them.

It's not a pretty job that we have. Mike Rowe would be at home here. Saltwater and sea creatures have a way of changing the appearance of the human form. We've seen some pretty gruesome stuff out here; bodies bloated so badly by water saturation and sun exposure that they look on the verge of exploding; limbs lost to large marine predators; faces so badly picked at by small parasites that dental records are needed to conclusively identify the victim.

As I continue to peer forward, I can see out of the corner of my eye where my Wayfarers don't cover, Scott is stretching out and reaching toward the body. As he does so, he pulls himself quickly away from it bolting upright in the boat. "Whoa!" he says looking down at the dead body of a small male, dark skin stained white in places by the salt and the sun. "We need to call for the Sheriff's patrol," he says.

"Why is that?" I ask fully turning my head now from the bow to the form in the water. For the first time I am seeing it as a human body instead of simply as a target that needs recovering. That's when I see it. In the center of the forehead is a ragged circle, bloated and erupting outward due to the time in the water.

"Is that a bullet hole?" I ask Scott.

"I do believe so," he answers as he begins to put on his protective gear. In addition to a full body wetsuit including gloves, Scott also dons his flippers, mask and snorkel, and adds over his wetsuit a flotation device that allows him to regulate his buoyancy by blowing into a tube. With the boat dead in the water (that's still funny to me), Scott lowers himself gently into the water using the grab rail that is mounted on the outside of the hull of the Whaler. Yes, the rail is on the *outside* of the boat, and not because I mounted it there.

My Whaler isn't just another vessel; no Boston Whaler is. But mine is special among Whalers too. *Recovery* is her name and like all Whalers, she is a direct descendant of the original unsinkable legend that Dick Fisher built in 1958. You may have seen the pictures or even a video of a Whaler cut in three pieces, all of which float, the one with the motor still operational as a vessel. But *Recovery* has some upgrades.

She is a retired United States Navy 1998 Guardian, twenty-five feet in length and re-powered with twin 150 horsepower Honda four-stroke outboards. The original Guardians were basically a stock Outrage or Montauk model hull that was reinforced for workboat use, fire and police, and for the military, like mine. This one was used specifically for delivering and recovering special forces in shallow water. Rigid Inflatable Boats - you've probably heard them called RIBs - are used for this as well, but the Whaler gives more stability, can't be punctured and is unsinkable. The reinforced hulls are rated to take 1,000 rounds from enemy fire and stay afloat. I'm not sure who tested that. The grab rails on the outside are designed as hand holds for warriors to lower themselves in or pull themselves out of the water, and sometimes for them to hold on to underway if a rapid exit from enemy combatants is necessary.

The name *Recovery* has multiple meanings. One of them is obvious already; she recovers the dead from the sea. The other is more personal as I am a recovering alcoholic. The name reminds me today and every day that I am never healed of my disease, that I am always in recovery; I also find myself almost every day in *Recovery*, whether collecting a body from the sea or just running up and down our shores. Perhaps it's why I chose the business I am in. It's a far cry from what I used to be.

Chapter 3

After college at East Carolina University and a degree in Communications Arts, I began business life as a graphic designer and copywriter at a small advertising agency in Charlotte. The agency focused me mainly on automotive at first and, as it turned out, I was pretty good at it, at least in the North Carolina market. If you are going to be in the advertising business though, there is no place like New York. I sent my portfolio off to Ogilvy and after two trips for multiple-day interviews, I was offered an assistant creative director position and moved to New York City.

Once in the Big Apple I improved my craft working with some of the best in the world, and I was able to move up in the industry by moving to different agencies. With each move I was able to increase my pay. Some would say my ego was also getting larger as my wallet did. I am to this day amazed at what they paid me to spout the ideas that were in my head. In any other business I would have been fired and perhaps even arrested for lewd and lascivious behavior.

Alcohol fueled my brain. When I got short on ideas, a cigarette and a shot were just the thing to jumpstart thought again. And it became more and more necessary as time went on. The thing is, my employer noticed, but didn't really care. I was the rainmaker. My ideas created billing. My ideas sold product. My ideas kept clients happy and had more wanting our agency to represent them. But my body couldn't keep up with my habits.

At thirty-four I had my first heart attack. I was lucky that I lived in New York City because I was on my way home in a taxi instead of behind the wheel of my own car. The cabby took me directly to Mount Sinai Medical Center where I was immediately wheeled into the emergency room in severe cardiac distress. They were able to save me, and my doctor set out a nutrition and exercise program for me that was designed to save my life. It did not include alcohol. At the time, alcohol wasn't only my fuel, it was my fun too. Life without fuel and fun didn't appeal to me so I ignored my doctor's orders.

My creative mind was better than ever. I was promoted to Chief Creative Officer for the Americas and almost doubled my income. That meant more money for fuel and fun. Over the next year I won a couple national Addy's, the awards the advertising business gives to you when you are at the top of the heap that they determine. I was highlighted in *AdAge* and *Advertising Week*. I was the guy you wanted to have driving the creative for your ad campaign. I was now one of the best in the world. I was, that is, until my second heart attack at thirty-eight.

This time I was drunk and at home and found unconscious by my cleaning lady approximately four hours later. In some ways, closing the bars down at 4am helped me that day. I was again rushed to Mount Sinai, but this time in an ambulance.

Miraculously, they were able to save me, but you probably guessed that already.

Three days later I returned to my apartment in the Murray Hill neighborhood on the midtown east side of Manhattan. I once again had the diet and activity schedule from my doctor. I looked it over with new eyes this time, and it seemed that, regardless of the fuel I needed and the fun I wanted, he might have a point. I had been rewarded handsomely for drinking over the years, so I truly could not see a way to stop, and I feared that I wouldn't be able to write again.

I went to a "celebrity" rehab in Delray Beach, Florida because the agency required it, and because they paid the bill. I also felt that I met the criteria, other than the alcoholic thing of course. While I had the best of intentions when I arrived, it didn't take long before I decided that I didn't belong there. All these people around me were screwed up. I didn't want to be around them.

I left rehab and hit the town in Delray. If you've never been there, Delray Beach is one of the coolest little towns in America. It is also the absolute worst place for an alcoholic. Great

18

bars, funny bartenders and beautiful women are not a recipe for a successful rehab, and so mine was over.

At the end of one night after a successful round of drinking and an unsuccessful round of finding female companionship, I went out to the beach and fell asleep. I don't remember doing it. I do remember waking up with the sun shining directly into my face, the glare hurting my head. I was covered in ant bites, which, as it turns out, I am allergic to. As I am sitting there unable to do much, a police officer came up to me and tried to talk with me. I couldn't respond to him. He assumed I was drunk, which I was, but he also saw the rash on my body and called an ambulance. They rushed me to Bethesda Medical Center in Boynton Beach.

I went into shock at some point during all of this and the next thing I remember is waking in a hospital bed almost two days later. I'd love to tell you that my family or friends were there to welcome me back into the world, but that's not the case. I was alone. For the third time before my fortieth birthday my life needed to be saved. Not because I was an adrenaline junky or worked in a dangerous job, but because of the personal decision I made to drink alcohol. I returned to the rehab center and stayed off Atlantic Avenue for the remainder of my time in Delray Beach.

I returned to my apartment in New York City and nothing felt the same.

I was healthier than I had been in almost fifteen years, and my place in Manhattan just wasn't my home anymore. It says a lot about your personal relationships when your housekeeper is the only person who checks on you after you return from rehab. In fact, it was Sonia who removed all the alcohol from my home before I came back.

I was done with New York. I worked with my employer to take early retirement and we settled on a nice exit package and an agreement that included me not holding them responsible for contributing to my problem by ignoring and profiting from it. I put my apartment up for sale and when it sold, I returned to the North Carolina Outer Banks where I spent my youth. My first day home I was walking around the Shallowbag Bay Marina down the road from my childhood home in Manteo and saw a forty-three-foot motor yacht for sale. I should mention that "motor yacht" is the model, not a pretentious or snooty reference to a boat. And while I agree that she is simply a boat, she is a Hatteras, which *does* make her better than other vessels her age and size.

The yacht – I mean boat – looked to be in pretty good condition, so I inquired. I bought her, rented the slip she was in, and she and the Outer Banks are now my home. I set up a small office in the salon on the back of the galley counter, and I write almost every day. I am trying to write a novel and so I named the Hatteras *First Draft*. I also rent the slip next door where I dock *Recovery*.

You may wonder how I got into the business of recovering dead bodies from the sea. Pretty simple really. I saw a business one day that specialized in cleaning up crime scenes, specifically gruesome murder sites. It was kind of like Merry Maids on steroids and carrying a whole lot more bleach. My first thought was, *if someone makes money by doing that, I wonder if I could make money by recovering bodies at sea?* Wouldn't everyone think of that? Apparently not, and so I filled a need for the Sheriff's office in Dare County. And there was no alcohol involved in that idea.

Honestly though, it pays well when they need me, keeps costs down for the Sheriff's Department, and it keeps me on the waters of the Outer Banks. The sea, the wind and the sound of my Whaler motoring through the bay or ocean are my new fuel and fun.

Chapter 4

The Sheriff's boat is approaching quickly from the south but slows long before it reaches us. I had radioed earlier that we had a homicide victim, not an accident victim, and was told that a Sheriff's Deputy was being dispatched to our location. I was also directed to do nothing until they got here.

Sheriff's Deputy Majik has a long history with these waters and is one of the best Captains I know. She is also the only Dare

County Sheriff that regularly runs the Department center console, so I was anticipating her arrival. She slows her vessel a couple hundred yards short of us. This eliminates her wake which in this case is more than a courtesy; it also lessens the chance that any evidence on the body will be disturbed.

As she nears my attention is no longer on the dead body, but instead on the very live body of Deputy Majik. She stands about five foot four inches tall, her long dark hair is in a ponytail that is then folded back into itself a few times to create a winding bun just to the back of the top of her head, hanging out through the back of her Dare County Sheriff's Department hat. Her shirt is the same light tan as the street cops wear in our warm Carolina summers, but hers is made by Performance Gear and resembles the fishing shirts most of the charter Captains wear. Like the one I'm wearing too. She has shorts on instead of uniform pants and her tan over her already darker, Indian skin accentuates the muscles in her thighs and calves. Although her uniform hides it well, you can tell that she is fit and has curves in all the right places. Deputy Majik idles to a stop on my port side, throws a couple fenders over her gunwale and deftly takes the lines I offer her to tie the patrol boat tight against *Recovery*.

Zaina Majik grew up in this area just like I did, only ten years after me. Her parents emigrated from India to the United States when she was five, and while her parents remained traditional Indian parents, Zaina is an all-American girl.

She grew up as what can only be described as a "tomboy." She loved to ride her bike, swim, fish, and most, to run the little Carolina Skiff her father had behind their house on the Croatan Sound. Incredibly inquisitive, Zaina would explore from sunup to sundown during summers, pulling the skiff into small tributaries barely wide enough for the boat. She would fish the shallows near the shorelines bringing all sorts of live and dead creatures home for further exploration. To her parents' credit, they supported her in all her endeavors and never once restricted her growth into an Indian-blooded American girl. At least not until she became interested in law enforcement.

Long family conversations were had over the traditional Thali dinner served in Katrori bowls. "You cannot be a policeman Zaina. It is too dangerous." her mother would say in her soft voice. "We implore you, be an accountant or manage a business Zaina! You will make more money!" her father would say more

24

sternly. But, being Zaina, her mind was made up. And so here she is.

"Hey Coop," she says. "What you got here?"

Her voice shakes me from my thoughts. I return to the present situation and remember that Scott is in the water holding onto a murder victim so that the body doesn't float away on the tide.

"Hey Magic, I hope you are well," I say. I have always given the people I know nicknames, the ones I like get good ones. I like Zaina and her last name made this an easy one. Ma-JEEK became MA-jik. She likes it and I am glad.

"Looks like this guy won't have any water in his lungs," I say. "Come on aboard and take a look." Magic expertly steps over the gunwales of the boats into *Recovery*, she walks around the stern side of the helm seat and looks down into the water.

"Hey Scotty. How you doin' down there?"

"Well Magic, I'm doin' just fine," Scott says in his slow Louisiana drawl not taking his eyes off the body. "This guy, however, not so much. Male, approximately mid to late twenties, dark skin, small caliber gunshot wound to the forehead, no exit wound so the bullet's probably still in there. He is certainly *not* the kid we thought he was."

Scotty and I were sent out to recover a missing teen who was on vacation in Kitty Hawk. He was thrown from one of those rent-by-the-hour deathtraps called "personal watercraft" and has been missing for over 24 hours. This is the kind of calls we normally get. The fishing boat that discovered the body floating called it into the police and they called us. Now we are talking about homicide. How quickly my world changes sometimes.

"Have you touched anything?" Magic asks.

"Nothing without gloves on. I turned him over originally and have been holding on to his left arm keeping him company in the water since."

"Okay. Crime scene divers should be here to relieve you shortly. Thanks Scotty."

"It's my pleasure ma'am," Scott replies as though he has just served her a drink on a cruise ship.

Scott Parker grew up in Mandeville Louisiana, a tiny town in St. Tammany Parish on the north shore of Lake Pontchartrain. He is a descendant of the Prieto family whose ancestry can be traced all the way back to the founding of the town in 1834. As most kids that grew up in the Bayou of Louisiana, Scotty was an adventurer. He loved the water and had no fear. On the lake almost every day of his young life, Scott learned to swim early and never stopped.

He swam competitively in High School and was noticed by college scouts. Among many offers, Scott chose the Coast Guard Academy in New London, Connecticut. Afterall, if you are going to swim in college, why not for a service that protects the waters and coastlines of the United States. After graduation, Scott moved on to Rescue Swimmer school in Elizabeth City, North Carolina, just miles up the Pasquotank River from where we are right now. Since then he has never left this area working in these waters for the Coast Guard, and now for me. Whether it is his upbringing or his training, Scott is one of the most easy-going people I have ever met. Wading in the waters off the Outer Banks holding on to a dead body, Scott looks just as relaxed as he does when we go diving on our day off.

The crime scene team doesn't have their own boat, so they catch a ride with one of the local fishing guides. Calling Brian DeForge a fishing guide is generous. He has a boat and a Captain's license but that is about the extent of it. He certainly boats and has lines in the water *near* fish, but few make it into his boat. As a Captain, his skills are lacking and he comes roaring in too close pushing a wake into our boats making them rock. He finally gets his boat situated on the far side of Magic's and yells over, "How are you today Cap?" He likes to call other boat Captain's, "Cap," in hopes that they will call him the same.

"What's happening Kermit?" I told you about nicknames and how they reflect my feelings about people. Change a couple letters around in his last name and you have DeFrog, thus Kermit. Yes, I know I can be an asshole sometimes. You can guess how I feel about Brian DeForge.

Kermit talks some more but I'm not listening. I'm watching as the crime scene techs work in the water for just a few minutes, and then arrange to have the body lifted onto *Recovery*. Once on-board, the techs spend more time taking samples and swabbing parts of the body before sealing it into a body bag with evidence tape over the zipper. They then load the body into the coffin box I installed on the deck of the Whaler for just this purpose. It's not a coffin, it's just the name used to describe the type of deck box that is similar in size and shape to one.

Magic thanks the techs for their work, they say their "Goodbyes," to each of us and they are quickly motoring back toward shore with Captain Kermit.

"I'll follow you in and the coroner's van will be waiting at the ramp," Magic tells me as she unties her boat, pulls in her fenders and casts off.

I nod my head and reply, "See you there Magic."

Chapter 5

I am not normally in a rush when on the Whaler but today I use much of the horsepower *Recovery* has and cruise south down Roanoke Sound and under Highway 64 that carries cars east and west between Roanoke Island, home to the towns of Manteo and Wanchese, and Nags Head's Pond Island, the gateway to North Carolina's Outer Banks. The coroner's van is waiting at the end of the service road that runs adjacent to the south side of the

Washington Baum Bridge. It has backed in as other trucks do, as though it too is waiting to drag a boat out of the water. This van, however, has no trailer hitch. On both sides of the black van the word *'Coroner'* is stenciled in reflective gold with a white drop shadow, in the same font as all of Dare County Sheriff's vehicles. Its back doors are closed and as we idle closer to the dock, I can see one passenger through the driver-side window. The engine running, condensation from the air conditioner is dripping underneath the vehicle and pooling on the pavement. Fishermen and other bystanders are looking curiously at the out of place van.

The man in the driver seat turns toward the window and sees us pulling up with Magic right behind us. Doc Watson - his real name - steps out of the driver side door and walks to the back. A tech named Theodore hops out of the other side and eagerly meets the Doc at the rear of the van. He opens the barn doors and reaches in for the gurney, pulling it out onto the ramp. Now we really have everyone's attention. If a van marked with the word *Coroner* didn't get it already, an empty gurney pulled from that van now does. I suppose pulling an empty gurney from a van labeled *Bakery* would have the same result.

I call the tech '*Beav*,' short for *Eager Beaver* and a nod to his television namesake, "Theodore Beaver Cleaver." You may think that I don't like Beav or that his nickname is a slight of some kind, but I assure you neither is the case. First, he does a job that few would want to do, and he obviously has a passion for it. Second, even more than his first name, I can't help but equate his small-town "Aw, shucks," demeanor to that of the Beav, and I loved that show as a kid. It was in re-runs and such a throwback to its time that I couldn't help but wish I were part of his world. Our present-day Beav rolls the gurney toward the dock, nodding toward me and Scott, the coroner leading the way and greeting us with a quick wave.

"Hey there Coop. I hear you have a delivery for me," the Doc says in his coastal Carolina accent, stepping from the pavement and onto the dock.

Doc Watson is in his late 60s and looks more like Colonel Sanders of Kentucky Fried fame than Doctor Mallard from *NCIS*; and he makes a mean barbecue chicken, so perhaps he is closer in personality to the Colonel as well. He's just over six feet tall, stocky to the heavy side with a white mustache and beard, white hair curling out from under his Dare County Sheriff's Department cap. He is wearing a dark jump suit with the Dare County logo on the left breast, and "Dr. Mitchell Watson, Coroner" stitched on the other. He has an easy style about him, with a quick wit that leans sarcastic.

"I sure do Doc," I say. I know, not the most creative nickname for a Doctor; it's been done. But I like the man and "Mitch," or "Banjo," just doesn't fit him. He has a presence that one can only acquire from decades of experience. He has earned the title and he deserves to be addressed by it.

We are tied off on the south side of the northern-most dock as Magic secures the Sheriff's Department center console to the next pier south. She ties it quickly and walks over to give Doc official details.

"Coop and Scott thought they were recovering the teen that's been missing since yesterday. Instead they picked up what looks to be a Hispanic or light-skinned black male with a bullet hole in the center of his forehead. Let's get him back and see what you can learn, okay Doc?"

"Sounds good to me," he replies.

Scott and I lift the bag out of the coffin box and lay it and its cargo on the starboard gunwale of the boat parallel to the dock. Magic and the Beav reach down and take the ends of the bag as Scott and I hand them up. Doc Watson is standing on the other side of the gurney to make sure it doesn't slip or tip over as Magic and the Beav place the bag as gently as possible onto the gurney. I step up onto the dock.

"I'll get him into autopsy and will let you know what I find," Doc says.

"Thanks Doc," Magic and I say at the same time. We look at each other a bit surprised. I keep forgetting that I am not an actual police officer. I keep thinking of Magic out of her uniform. It's all so confusing.

Chapter 6

Scott is sitting across from me in a window booth at Duke's Diner in Manns Harbor on highway 64 just across the Virginia Dare Memorial Bridge from Manteo to the east. Duke, the owner, is a childhood friend of mine but the diner isn't named for him, it's named for his father, also Duke, who started it back when we were kids. I jokingly used to call my friend "*Number Two*," as he was technically the second Duke in the family. He didn't like that much and so we settled on "*Junior.*"

Duke is a big guy, thick around the center, but still solid with significant muscle mass under, as his wife says, a couple layers of love. He played football in high school and then at Catawba College in Salisbury, North Carolina, but never graduated, returning home in the middle of his junior year when his dad got sick. He helped keep the restaurant alive, but unfortunately couldn't do the same for his father. Junior took over the restaurant when his dad died two years later, and he has been here ever since.

In recent years Junior has had his own health issues. Two years ago, he was diagnosed with stage 4 renal cancer that spread to his right lung, his liver, and at least one of his lymph nodes. After seven surgeries, radiation, chemo, immuno- and physical therapy, he has never lost his zest for life. His most recent scans are all clear, and the doctor that told him to get his affairs in order just two years ago had the pleasure of reversing that decision. More accurately he smiled when Duke said, "So I guess you were wrong then." Duke is a survivor, and he has cooked in this diner for the better part of two decades.

We spent a lot of time here as kids, especially in high school when we had our own cars and could drive ourselves. We used to have to take the Manns Harbor bridge from the north before the Dare Bridge was complete. It was a longer ride, but always worth it. In this very booth I have done homework, held hands with my first crush, joked with friends after a high school Friday night football games and written my first ad copy. "Eat at Duke's and you'll never puke." Admittedly, my writing career got off to a rough start.

We are the only people in the place except for one booth at the other end of the restaurant. There are three men, all Hispanic. The two that share the side closest to us are obviously laborers. Both men are short, around five foot four or five, and they are dressed in work boots, worn blue jeans, and tee shirts that were once white but are now stained with dust and sweat. They have removed their caps and their hair is messy and damp, their skin dark by heritage, made even darker by the sun.

The man across from them couldn't be more different. He is taller, close to six feet. He wears dress jeans that look new, cowboy boots that are shined to a clean, matte finish, a starched white collared button-down shirt with a black bolo tie, and a big, black cowboy hat that George Strait might wear. His skin is dark, but not singed by the sun like the other two. He also wears a scowl and seems to be interrogating the men across from him. I immediately don't like him. I dub him "*Bad Hombre.*"

"Who are those guys Number Two?" I ask Junior under my breath when he arrives with our food. I just can't help but use his old nickname.

"I don't know Poop, first time I've seen them," he replies. Now you know why I really stopped calling him Number Two.

"Poop?" Scott asks.

"Long story," we both say at the same time.

"That one guy irks me a bit," Junior continues. "He dresses a bit flashy for the beach, and he didn't even have the decency to take off his hat. He's not being very nice to those other two either."

"You understand Spanish Duke?" Scott asks.

"Not a word," he replies.

"Then how do you know he's not being nice?" Scott follows up.

"Look at him Scotty. You can read it on his face, in his expressions."

Scott looks over a bit more closely until the big guy notices. Scott looks away as though he hadn't been staring and whispers under his breath, "I see what you mean."

"Are you two girls done?" I ask. "Can we eat now?"

"Whatever Coop," Junior says in his gruff voice. He pulls up a chair from the table behind him, spins it around and sits down backwards on it at the end of our booth, his arms over the back rest facing the window. "So, what's been happening?" he asks. "I heard you had a floater yesterday."

"Yep," I say. "We thought we were headed out to find that teen that was lost off of Kitty Hawk on Sunday, but we got a bit of a surprise."

"What happened?"

Scott picks up the story in his slow, Louisiana drawl. "Well Duke, we idled up to the body like we always do. I looked over the side and noticed that this wasn't no teenage boy. It was a small man with a bullet hole between his eyes."

"How did that happen?" Junior asks.

"Probably with a gun," I respond.

"Fuck you Coop," Junior replies as only a friend of thirty years can.

"We don't know," Scott continues. "Doc Watson took the body back to do an autopsy."

"We'll know more tomorrow," I say.

"We?" Scott asks, a smirk on his face. "You do know that we aren't police, right?"

"Of course I do, but inquiring minds and all that. I want to know what happened."

Junior looks back toward the kitchen and seems to remember that he isn't a guest, he's the owner. Standing, he grabs the backrest of the chair spinning and skidding it back into position at the table it came from. "Well, keep it safe out there, as they say," Junior says trying to imitate Captain Frank Furillo from *Hill Street Blues*. I want to tell him that the line is, "Let's be careful out there," but I let it go.

Across the restaurant, Bad Hombre starts paying attention to the conversation as he overhears one of the men at the other table mention the body with a bullet hole in its head. He looks at the two men across the table from him and covertly motions to the door. They all stand up and walk toward the exit, Bad Hombre dropping a twenty-dollar bill on the register to cover their seventeen-dollar meal. One of the two laborers turns as they are walking out and catches the eye of the man sitting in the window booth wearing the short-sleeve fishing shirt. They nod to each other in passive greeting as passersby do. The three men walk into the parking lot and load into Bad Hombre's Mercedes.

Chapter 7

Bad Hombre's real name is Oscar, and Oscar is not happy. He is pacing angrily in front of Miguel and Hector who are bound with rope to folding chairs in the middle of small, detached garage on a remote property. Miguel has never been here before and he is not sure if he could find it again even if he tried. The circuitous route Oscar took to get here was meant to hide the location, and it succeeded. Near the end of the trip they drove across a short bridge that spanned a river, and Miguel feels certain that they are north of Albemarle Sound. Once they hit the dirt roads though, he lost any sense of direction that he had.

Miguel inspects his situation. The rope is wrapped around him tightly, encircling his upper arms, securing them against his body which is secured to the back of the chair. The line is long, and it continues under the seat and over his thighs twice, and then around his wrists binding them together. The line is then pulled straight down between his knees and tied somewhere he cannot see underneath the seat of his chair. He looks to his right and sees Hector is tied in a similar manner. The man who was waiting for them here certainly knows his knots.

"Tell me what happened!" Oscar demands, spittle flying from the corners of his mouth. "You were to dispose of the body at sea! Can I not trust you to do anything right!" He backhands Hector across the face and then steps aggressively toward Miguel, bending down and putting his head so close that Miguel smells stale cigarette smoke on his skin, and can feel the heat of his breath. "You call yourself a Captain?" Oscar taunts. Miguel does not respond. Instead, he stays eerily composed considering the circumstances.

44

Hector is crying hysterically, his body convulsing as he sobs. If he weren't tethered to the chair he would collapse onto the floor. Tears are flowing from his eyes and draining through his nose making their way into his mouth. His words are difficult to understand as he divulges all that happened a couple nights earlier.

"The boat... it seenking Jefe!" Hector cries in accented English using the Spanish word for 'boss.' "Agua... Water come in... and take heem! We look and look pero no find!" Hector is struggling for air through a windpipe clogging with his own tears, a wet cough expelling moisture like a drowning man breaking the surface after being submerged too long. "I am sorry Jefe!" he says looking up at Oscar for a moment, and then letting his head fall, his chin hitting his chest stopping its progress. He is staring at his lap, his shoulders shaking with each sob.

"Look at me!" Oscar says angrily. Hector keeps his head down unable to hear Oscar through his own bawling. "LOOK! AT! ME!" Oscar says loudly now, pronouncing each word separately, and stepping closer to Hector.

Hector looks up at him, mouth wide as he cries loudly, a real-life embodiment of the Edvard Munch painting, *The Scream.* Oscar bends down and removes a revolver from a holster at his ankle. He steps closer to Hector's chair and points it directly into the crying man's face. "Shut up!" he says.

Hector can't stop, tears flowing from his eyes, his mouth wide open, weeping. Fear has taken over and a loud sob that is almost a scream is all that comes out.

Hector clicks back the hammer on the revolver, raising the barrel higher taking aim just a few inches away from Hector's face. "SHUT! UP!" he says more loudly.

Hector is trying to find words to defend himself but what comes out is a screeching sound, the unintelligible hymn of a dying man instead of the request for mercy it is intended to be.

BAM! Oscar pulls the trigger striking Hector between his eyes. Hector's head snaps back, the energy of the gunshot and the weight of his body tipping the chair backwards onto the floor, Hector still secured to it. It is eerily quiet now that Hector can no longer make a sound. Gun smoke hangs in the air with the smell of gun powder and fresh blood. The only sound in the room is the whirring of a portable fan in the corner.

"Jefe..." Miguel tries to speak now.

"No!" Oscar stops him, abruptly turning and placing the hot muzzle of the revolver against Miguel's neck, searing his skin. Miguel doesn't make a movement or a sound. With the gun still against Miguel's neck, Oscar leans his face very close to Miguel's ear.

Oscar whispers, "No more mistakes. The next time it will be your daughter you will watch die, comprende?"

"Si," is all Miguel can say, thinking of his beautiful daughter. He hopes she is safe. He hopes she is being taken care of. He doesn't dare speak out knowing that her life is in Jefe's hands. *Soon this will be over*, he thinks to himself. He closes his eyes and offers a silent prayer to God.

Chapter 8

The next day I am leaving the diner after yet another meal at my childhood haunt. It's a beautiful sunny day, a bit warm but cooled somewhat by the sea breeze that is almost constant on the Outer Banks. I am thinking about the man Scott and I recovered as my phone rings in my back pocket. I pull it out and look at the screen. Seeing the name, I smile. I swipe the green circle right and answer, "You must have been reading my mind. What's up Magic?"

"Reading your mind? What?" she replies.

"Nothing… what can I do for you?"

"Doc Watson is completing his autopsy," she replies. "Can you meet me at his office in thirty minutes?"

"Sure," I reply, somehow excited by the possibility of seeing her, albeit at a morgue. "I'm still not a cop, you know," I add, a smile in my voice.

"And you never will be," Magic says matter-of-factly. "I am aware of that Coop. Everyone is aware of that." I can almost see her rolling her eyes. "Since you recovered him, I want you there in case I have any questions."

"Alright. I'll see you there," I answer trying to hide my disappointment. Somewhere in my twisted mind I guess I was hoping she wanted more than answers.

I turn right off highway 64 onto Marshall C. Collins Drive and into the parking lot of the Dare County Government offices. I pass the courthouse and continue around the Sheriff's Office building to the back of the property. I see Magic's Sheriff's Office Tahoe sitting in one of the official vehicle spaces close to the building. I park at the back of the lot, get out of my truck and walk across the hot blacktop toward her vehicle. As I get close, Magic opens her door and jumps out.

"I've never been to Doc's office. Where are we going?" I say in lieu of greeting.

"The basement," she replies. From every cop show I have ever watched I already knew that this was going to be her answer. As I turn to point that out to her, Magic holds one hand up in front of my open mouth, points toward the door with the other and simply says, "Don't."

The elevator opens into a small hallway. The walls and floors are white, lit generously by fluorescent tubes under checkered plastic covers that are inset into a hung ceiling. One

about ten feet down the hall seems to have a tube out and it creates
a dim shadow on the left side of the corridor. Passing it, the hallway
is fully lit again, and I see the placard next to the door on our right;
"Coroner." Magic turns the knob without knocking and we enter
Doc Watson's office.

The office is much the same as the hallway, white walls,
bright florescent lights and a single desk at the back of the room
where the Doc sits concentrating on a document laying in front of
him. There is a door behind him labeled "Exam 1." I look for
another door marked "Exam 2" but don't see one and wonder if it
exists. *Why would they use the number 1 if there is no number 2?*
I ask myself. My mind is wandering because I am nervous. I have
seen dead bodies often in the work I do but this office has me
rattled. I don't know the protocol here so I wait for someone else
to talk first, a rarity some might say.

"Hey Coop, Welcome to the underworld," Doc says,
looking up from the document and getting to his feet. "Let's step
inside," he adds as he sweeps his right arm and hand toward the
door behind his desk as if saying, '*After you.*'

Magic and I enter the small room and stand close to the door. Exam 1 is smaller than I would have expected for an autopsy room and I wonder if Exam 2 is any bigger; that is, of course, if it exists at all. My real-life experience with autopsy rooms is lacking in that I have seen exactly one as of today, so I rely on my copious cop show consumption to pass judgement on its accommodations.

The room has all the items I have seen in coroner's exam rooms on television and I find some comfort that the shows' producers have taken time to get it right. There are stainless steel medical counters around two walls, each drawer underneath neatly labeled. There is a light above an exam table. It is mounted on a telescopic arm that can be moved closer to a subject for more direct examination if it is needed. It is off right now, illumination in the room coming from lights mounted under the cabinets above each countertop. Oh, and there is the body of a small human under a sheet on the table. Did I forget to mention that?

Doc Watson picks up a folder from the counter near the foot of the exam table and puts his spectacles on. They are the type that hang from a lanyard around your neck, separate in the center of the bridge connected only by a magnet, and they 'click' when you put them back together above your nose. I make a mental note to get some of them for myself. He looks down at the body and then back to us.

"In case it wasn't obvious, cause of death is a gunshot wound to the head. There is no water in his lungs, so he was dead before he hit the water. His body was pretty badly picked at by sea life, so I took a lot of time on abrasions to determine what was post-mortem and what happened before he died."

"Was he beaten before being shot?" Magic asks.

"No, more like he was chased before someone caught him and then shot him," the coroner responds.

A look of confusion on my face, I speak for the first time. "Wait, what? He was chased? How can you possibly know that?"

Doc walks over to the table and turns on the exam lighting and a television screen that I hadn't noticed hanging in the corner. Standing beside the table he lifts the sheet exposing the left arm and rib cage of the body. He lowers one of the pieces of equipment from the ceiling and looking up at the TV screen, locates an injury on the body with the camera.

"You see all of these lines going in the same direction?" He says. I nod as he continues, "These are all over his upper torso and legs, and all go in the same direction, from front to back. Some are deeper and thicker than others so while they all probably happened during the same event, they did not all happen with the same instrument."

"How do you know they happened before he was shot?" I ask.

"Because there is blood in the wounds. A dead man wouldn't have bled if, say the body was dragged after he was killed. But there's more," Doc says as he covers the body back up and walks to a tray that is sitting on the other countertop. "I was able to pull fibers out of his hands and out of the wounds on his body. There were two in-particular, one a mystery and another that tells more of a story."

I stay quiet as does Magic. We are both engrossed by the Doctor's words. He truly is a great storyteller. Perhaps he should have thought about a career in country music.

"On his hands and arms there are textile fibers that are consistent with those found in older mattresses."

"What does that mean?" I ask.

"That is still a mystery to me right now. If they were just in his hands, he could have been moving mattresses without gloves, but in his arms and shoulder too? Perhaps sleeping on an exposed mattress, but that I don't know yet."

"And the one that tells more of a story?" Magic prompts.

"Yes," Doc says as he pulls the camera over to the tray he has placed on a rolling table. Items that look like big sticks are revealed on the television screen. "Each of these was found in one of the wounds on his body and every one of these wounds is moving from the front of his body toward the back." He moves the camera to reveal a few more items and these are easily identifiable as thorns and I am starting to get the picture.

"So, what you are saying is that he suffered these wounds while running through some brush. How do you know he wasn't a landscaper?" I challenge.

"Because none of these wounds had begun the healing process. They are all new and are just before his death. He was running from something through thick brush, and by the types of wood and thorns it was in the pine brush up along the shoreline of the Albemarle or one of the rivers. He was moving with little concern for his body."

"Somebody was chasing him." I state.

"Somebody was hunting him," Magic adds grimly.

"Precisely," the Doc says. "He was running away from something and someone."

"Not fast enough," I say.

Chapter 9

Later that evening I am reading below deck in the salon of my home, my 43-foot Hatteras Motor Yacht, *First Draft.* "Permission to come aboard?" I hear from the dock at the stern of the boat. It's Magic. She's never been here before and I look around the room to make sure it is in order and there is nothing that will embarrass me. I can do that on my own.

"Permission granted," I say. "C'mon aboard Magic."

She is dressed in civilian clothes; shorts that show off her legs, a loose-fitting translucent, white blouse with three buttons at the top, two of them open showing the tan skin of her chest. She has a white spaghetti strap sleeveless shirt under the blouse which outlines her body in the light from the dock behind her. If she had shoes on when she arrived, they are gone, respecting the long-standing tradition of no shoes on a boat.

"Nice boat," she says as she looks around. I think to myself, *Yacht*, as I look around too just to be sure there isn't a stray pair of boxers drying on the back of a chair. I offer her something to drink.

"I could really use a beer," she says.

"Yeah... me too," I reply with a bit of unintentional longing in my voice. At that moment she realizes she has misspoken and looks at me with both sympathy and embarrassment.

She reaches out and touches my arm. Electricity shoots through me. "I'm sorry Coop. I wasn't thinking," she says looking into my eyes and meaning it. "Do you have a Coke?"

"Not a problem Magic, really," I say sincerely. This isn't my first rodeo.

"No Coke," I say. "We are way too close to New Bern to serve Coke!" I continue, referring to the North Carolina city where Pepsi was invented, ninety miles southwest of here on the Neuse River.

Magic looks at me, confusion on her face. "What?" she says, shaking her head. I forget that not everyone is a pop culture and advertising geek.

"Pepsi okay?" I ask.

"Great," she answers.

"One Pepsi coming up," I say as I step down to the galley and disappear behind the refrigerator door.

When I return, she is looking at my desk, my notebooks a scribble of jottings in my hand, laptop open, the bubbles of the screen saver blocking its content.

"What's all this?" she asks.

"Well, I was a writer once, so in my quote, retirement," I say making air-quotes, "I figured I might want to be one again, but this time for me, not for the man," I say, stressing the last part with some strange body language that probably looked more like jazz hands than 'the man.'

"You writing poetry?" Magic smiles, teasing me.

"I don't think anyone would want that," I say, laughing a bit. "Longer form."

"A book?"

"That's the goal. Not as easy as I thought it would be."

"You'll do great," she says, again, meaning it and looking directly into my eyes. I am getting lost for a moment before a look of understanding crosses her face. "Ah. *First Draft*," she says. "I get it now," she says realizing the name of my home has more than one meaning as well.

"Exactly. So, what brings you here?" I say handing her a can of Pepsi and a glass of ice. As she turns to sit, I shake my head like Spicoli in *Fast Times at Ridgemont High*, and think to myself, *get it together Cooper!* I feel as nervous as my first kiss in middle school. …Okay, high school, you got me.

"I can't get the guy you recovered out of my mind," she says. "It reminds me too much of my younger brother."

I knew Magic had lost a brother, but I couldn't recall any details. It happened in the time I was away from Manteo. Regardless of where I was physically, my mind and ego weren't in a place that I would have remembered anyway. I don't say a word, I just look at her as she peers down into her glass of Pepsi and rattles her ice. When she is finally ready, she tells the story.

Her brother Arjun was three years younger than her. Unlike Magic, Arjun didn't have an outlet for the teasing that comes with being a brown-skinned person in a mostly white small, southern town. While Magic would go off and fish and explore, Arjun would try to fit in and prove that he belonged. At some point he fell in with a group of kids who were also outcasts, but who had decided to deal with it through truancy and by consuming illicit substances.

Drug and alcohol-fueled teen angst gave way to petty theft, and a couple arrests. Due to his seemingly constant run-ins with the law, Arjun was always battling with his parents. They truly wanted to help him if they could. "Your name means 'courageous' Arjun, you can do this." his mother would say, her tone soft. "You must stop this behavior immediately!" his father would add with much more volume. But Arjun couldn't stop.

Arjun disappeared one fall day in his Junior year of high school while his sister was at the Police Academy in Winston-Salem, six hours to the west. Six months later just after her graduation, Arjun was found behind an ABC store in Raleigh, laying on an old mattress, beaten and dead. There were no leads and police didn't try very hard to pursue the killer or killers. What's one more brown-skinned druggy dead behind a strip mall? One fewer problem as far as the police were concerned.

Magic is moved greatly by telling this story and I begin to realize that she either doesn't tell it much, or perhaps has never told it before. She is quietly crying, tears escaping her eyes and running slowly down her face. I reach out and put my hand on her upper arm to offer some comfort. Magic leans her head over and presses her cheek against my hand, the wetness of her tears between our skin creating heat.

"I'm so sorry Zaina," I say, using her real name for the first time in forever. She looks up into my eyes.

"I don't want the same thing to happen now. I couldn't help Arjun. I can help this boy," she says. "No one is going to pursue this very hard. He lived on the margins. There are no leads; no missing person reports fit the victim. The detectives have nothing." Still looking into my eyes, she says, "Help me."

"How?" I ask.

"Let's start at the beginning. The GSW to the head is the finality for him, but what happened before and after that. Before we have abrasions from running through brush. You know the waters around here as well as I do... "

"You want to go looking around to see what we can find?" I say interrupting her.

Magic sits up straight and smiles. "I thought you would never ask," she says wiping tears away with the back of her hand.

"When?"

"Tomorrow's my day off," she says, still smiling.

I look at her. She is determined. She is beautiful. "It's a date," I say with a surrendering grin. Her face brightens with a bigger smile.

Outside of the window an old fishing boat is cruising by on the bay headed out to sea.

Chapter 10

"Here are the GPS coordinates. Go!" Oscar says to Miguel. They are on the Blackfin heading out toward Oregon Inlet. Oscar has brought a new first mate, a man that is unknown to Miguel. Oscar is along for this trip as well, the only time that has happened during Miguel's tenure as Captain. The new mate appears to be an able deckhand, but Miguel knows he is aboard for more than that. *Jefe feels he needs to keep an eye on me*, he thinks. Miguel enters the coordinates into the GPS as his new first mate peers at the screen over his shoulder.

Miguel steers the Blackfin thinking to himself about how he ended up here. *I just wanted a better life for my daughter*, he thinks to himself. *And for me.* He trusted the wrong man to get him and his family to the United States, and now he has to repay a debt to this criminal. *What's the English word?* he asks himself. *Coyote.* More like a Wolf waiting to pounce on the vulnerable, only dressed in cowboy clothing. He has difficulty doing the job he does, but what choice does he have? He rationalizes his situation by telling himself that he is simply transporting people to freedom. But he knows better.

He thinks about running for a moment. He can steer the boat in waves that will surely make Jefe sick and when he goes to the side to throw up, a little throttle and perhaps a shove is all it would take to send him toppling over the side. The man would not float long with those boots on. But the new first mate is on the boat as well, and Miguel knows this would never work. Causing one man to fall into the sea is difficult enough. Coordinating two accidents without assistance is not possible. And Jefe is still holding his daughter, Angela, his little angel. No, there is nothing he can do other than exactly what Jefe tells him to do. He thinks to himself, *only two more trips and I am paid in full and I will have my Angela back with me.* He worries, though, that Jefe will not honor his part of the deal, and that he will never see his daughter again.

The boat is late. The Blackfin sits in the dark at the coordinates Oscar gave Miguel, swaying side to side in rolling but manageable seas. Miguel knows he could make the wait much smoother by idling into the waves, but he takes some satisfaction in making Jefe uncomfortable.

Miguel sees the vessel's anchor light first, a small white dot bobbing toward them. As it gets closer, he can see its shape now, a small freighter with only one shipping container on it is motoring in from the south. The Captain of the other boat shifts its engine to neutral and drifts slowly to a stop. The freighter is boxy and made of steel, and the elements have taken a toll on its decks and wheelhouse. Rust covers every exposed area, and there are many where paint has long ago flaked off. It is a heavy vessel and the seas don't have the same effect as they do on the Blackfin. It rests almost completely level on the dark sea.

Miguel shifts into forward and steers the Blackfin up beside the freighter as he directs his first mate to put fenders out, and to get a spring line ready. The container is now open and at least twelve people walk out onto the salty deck, men, women and children. Miguel looks for a moment at one little girl and thinks that she might be his Angela. While she is about the same height and age, her hair is longer, and he knows it is not her. All of them are dirty and obviously exhausted after the trip inside of the hot container. Each is handed a water bottle but other than that it looks like there is nothing else left to eat or drink, empty water bottles litter the floor.

The container has come in from Jacksonville, FL where it was picked up by this freighter two days earlier. Prior to that it and its cargo endured a crossing of the Gulf of Mexico and then transport through the St. John's river up through Florida to a small shipping yard near the port of Jacksonville where the container was deposited to wait for pickup by this crew. The migrants walk out into the night and open air for the first time in a week, the stench of human waste obvious in the air. All are tired and some need

68

assistance, but all are alive, now floating on a barge somewhere out in the Atlantic Ocean off the coast of North Carolina.

Miguel turns the Blackfin's courtesy lights on to help the passengers see where they are stepping as they board. As they are transferred over the gunwale into the Blackfin, Miguel hands each an orange life jacket and explains how to put it on. He tries to look each in the eye as well, hoping they see and feel some friendship and compassion from him, perhaps the first they have experienced in weeks, and probably the last they will experience for a long time to come.

There is little room in the cabin once all are transferred, eight children and seven adults, fifteen in all. It is small, but at least there is dim light, water, and a struggling air conditioner powered by the boat's small generator. The new deckhand threatens the group in Spanish to stay below and to not move the blinds away from any windows. He closes the salon door, locking it from the outside. He ignores Miguel as he walks past him, stepping up to the bow to release the line tethering them to the freighter. Miguel does the same with the stern line and then climbs the ladder to the flybridge to get under way. The freighter crew releases the spring line and they are floating free again.

The plan is always to arrive in the dark. Since the freighter was running late, however, the Blackfin and its cargo are entering Oregon Inlet just before first light. Miguel captains the vessel north through Roanoke Sound passing Wanchese and Manteo to the east. He notices a small center console idling out of Shallowbag Bay with two passengers, a man and a woman. He continues north and then turns west in Albemarle Sound heading in the direction of Edenton. His destination is past that, up the Chowan River where he will transfer his passengers to land and trucks that will take them inland. A tear slowly makes its way down his cheek.

Chapter 11

As we head out at first light, there are just a few boats out on the bay. A couple center consoles are heading south rigged for a day of fishing. A smaller sportfish cruises by heading north riding a bit low in the water. *A good catch,* I think to myself.

"So, what are we looking for?" I ask. I know what I am looking *at*, and it is Magic, literally and figuratively. Her hair is up in a ponytail, but without the county Sheriff's hat that I normally see her in. She is wearing an army green bikini top that covers her medium sized breasts and captures my attention. She has on worn and hole-ridden, capri-length jeans over white bikini bottoms that peek up through her fly that is purposely left unbuttoned at the top. I think she does this to torture me. I like it.

"Areas in the shoreline that look disturbed. He was running through brush and branches shortly before he was murdered, and I have a hunch that the only way he would have escaped into them is by water. Anyone in pursuit would have been by boat and would have disturbed the growth while landing on shore."

"There are hundreds of miles of shoreline up these rivers. You know that better than anyone."

"I know," she says sliding out of her capri jeans. "I needed a break today anyway and a day on the water in a boat that doesn't say 'Sheriff' on it, and with my own personal Captain, is just what I need." Magic takes out her sunscreen and begins to apply it, first to her face, being diligent about covering any exposed skin. She then takes a separate bottle, squirts some into her hand. I'm sure there is a better word than 'squirts' but my vocabulary is escaping me at the moment. She spreads the lotion around with her other hand and then uses both to massage it into her arms, shoulders, back, stomach and then legs. I watch the entire spectacle feigning disinterest.

"A lot of places to hide," I say, hoping I am not drooling like a dog.

"Yep. I used to count on that as a kid. I'd get lost and fantasize about being Queen of all of this," she says as she sweeps her arms signifying the water and shoreline that surrounds us. "I would swim naked all the time."

"And where was I?" I think.

"Based upon what you told me last night, probably New York City getting drunk," she replies with a smile. Apparently, I didn't just think the question. I must stop doing that.

"Even at my worst, I always remembered how special this place is," I say, looking around at the peacefulness of it all. "It's why I returned. I don't think I could have made it anywhere else."

I am looking at where the water meets the shore. I look deeper and into my past. This was my home and my passion when I was young. All I ever wanted was to be out on these waters, to mess around with Junior and my other buddies. To watch girls in bikinis as they watched us, them giggling, us trying not to show our excitement. We didn't have a care in the world.

Then I think about my life as a big shot New York City creative director and copywriter and wonder how I lost my way. Sure, there are rewards to being in the advertising business. I partied with celebrities, been on the list at all the hot clubs and seen and heard my work on every mass medium, all over the world. But there are also things I will never remember because of the choices I made.

This is all I ever wanted, I think as I move my gaze along the shoreline. Breaking the trance I have been in, I turn to see Magic's compassionate eyes fixed on me. She gives me a knowing grin and puts her hand on my shoulder as though she can see what I am thinking.

"Let's concentrate on today, okay Coop?" she says, confirming my suspicion.

We search areas on the east and west shores of the Alligator River, heading down its tributaries, paying attention to shoreline in secluded areas that might have recently been struck by a boat. We peek up Mill Tail Creek, the water path to an old ghost town named Buffalo City. A bustling logging town in the early twentieth century, Buffalo City automated much of its process shipping logs by rail to Mill Creek, and then by barge down to the Alligator River and to the world. While most towns in North Carolina suffered terribly during the Great Depression, Buffalo City thrived by utilizing its processes to ship moonshine. It's hard to believe that what is now part of the Alligator River National Wildlife Refuge was once the largest settlement in Dare County.

We reach a southern tree line on the river and turn west, passing the manmade portion of the river that is the Intracoastal

Waterway and would lead us to the Pungo River. We decide that too many boats pass through this channel and we move on, farther west toward the Preyer Reserve.

By early afternoon we have found nothing, so we decide to break for lunch. I toss the anchor out, let the boat drift back on the breeze and current, and then tie it off to the bow cleat. Magic had the forethought to go to Publix in Kitty Hawk and fill a cooler with ice, subs and some drinks, I notice that she has Pepsi and not Coke and tip my hat in the direction of New Bern. We are sitting on top of the coffin box eating our sandwiches and drinking our sodas, each of our cans wrapped in *Recovery* koozies. Conversation is minimal as we eat, both content to sit quietly and take in our surroundings. It's a hot day. The air is mostly still down-river.

"I'm hot," Magic says. *Yes, you are,* I think. "I'm going swimming," she continues. I didn't say it out loud this time. I'm getting better.

Magic stands facing me, pausing for a moment, or maybe my brain is just slowing it down so I don't miss anything. She turns toward the port gunwale, her back to me now. She brings both her arms behind her, the back of her hands against her hips, puts her fingers inside the outer edges of her bottoms and runs them downward, freeing the fabric from between her cheeks. It is something all women seem to do and perhaps it has become so habitual they no longer realize that they do it. It gets me every time.

She steps up onto the gunwale and stands completely still for a moment, arms at her side, head upright and staring off into the distance. I can't help but admire her body, but I also wonder what she is thinking in that moment. I can barely see the profile of her face outlined by the sky, but in my mind, I can see her eyes, exploring and focused. She then bends her legs while swinging her arms back and then forward, and springs off the side, entering the water in a perfect dive, her athletic form slicing the water creating minimal splash. *Recovery* slides away from her in reaction to the force. For every action, there is a reaction they say. I can tell you that in response to Magic's action I am definitely having a reaction.

Magic surfaces and treads water about ten feet away from the boat. She opens her eyes, looks at me and says, "Come join me!" *Hmm, secluded spot, hot girl, water.* You don't have to ask me twice. I execute a less-than-elegant dive and come up just a couple of feet in front of Magic, facing her. She looks at me a moment, and then leans back going under the water, surfacing face first so her hair is slicked back, and then runs her hands over her hair smoothing it just to make sure. Her slender arms are above the water, tight muscle glistening in the sun as water runs off of them. This gets me every time too. A lot gets me every time. I am glad to be in the water at that moment because my interest is becoming noticeable just a couple feet below the surface.

"I thought you said you swim naked," I say, looking into her eyes.

"Not on a first date," she replies with a smile. She executes a perfect surface dive, swimming below me and surfacing at the stern of *Recovery*. She does that hair thing again, and then grabs the handles of the ladder and slowly brings herself out of the water, taking each step slowly, her hips shifting with each as she brings herself onto the dive platform. Damn. that gets me every time.

Chapter 12

Miguel is running the Blackfin slowly through a tight waterway, tangles of branches encroaching from both shorelines. He is in a tributary off the Chowan River and while he knows there is enough water, he checks the depth-finder anyway. He idles up to a worn out, secluded space in the brush that serves as a dock but is identifiable only as an abandoned and stuck railroad tie at the surface. There is decking behind that just below the waterline. It leads inland to a watery path, that takes his passengers to their next method of transport. Miguel knows there must be a roadway at the end of a path with a waiting vehicle large enough to transport his passengers, but this is the farthest he has ever been on this journey.

Miguel is below deck, his daughter Angela is sobbing into his chest, the boat rocking due to winds and rain that are pummeling the vessel. He is surrounded by ten others in including two of his friends and co-workers in Mexico, José and Hector. All the other passengers are Mexican as well, and Miguel can see the fear in their eyes. Boating is not something that many of them have experienced before and after this ride, few will ever want to again.

He hears shouts from the flybridge above the cabin. The boat begins to shift violently from side to side, passengers crashing into one another trying to keep their places but failing. The cabin door opens and the Captain steps in, misses the stairs and falls to the floor of the salon. He is bleeding badly from a gash above his right eye. The boat continues to sway, winding through the seas as whomever is running the boat now tries to recover control.

"Hector, put pressure on his wound," Miguel shouts. "José, come with me!" Miguel jumps up and is in the cockpit in seconds, rain blowing forcefully into his face. It is dark and that combined with the vessels unpredictable movement makes climbing to the flybridge difficult. Miguel crests the top of the ladder and finds the first mate trying to gain control but doing everything completely wrong. After fifteen years working as a Captain, Miguel knows a good seaman when he sees one, and this man is not one of them.

Miguel pushes the man aside and takes the wheel. He pulls back on the throttles and begins to turn to starboard. As the boat comes into the wind, Miguel pushes the throttles up just slightly to control the motion of the vessel. It moves up and down now moving into the waves and minimizing any side to side rolling.

"Where are we going?" he asks shouting the question at the first mate. The man is cowering down below the bulkhead of the helm and staring down into a lighted screen in his hand. Miguel grabs the device, a handheld GPS unit. Previous tracks are still on *the screen and Miguel notices that they are well off the path they should be on, and probably getting precariously close to shore. He steers the boat until he sees on the device that his path will intersect with the previous course on the screen. The wind is buffeting the vessel, but in Miguel's skilled hands, his passengers will be mostly comfortable.*

José is behind Miguel now and takes the GPS. As Miguel steers, José give him instructions on where to go, and keeps watch for any danger. Together they get the boat to a location that looks like nothing, just a railroad tie floating in the water close to the brush line that surrounds the waterway.

"We walk from here," the first mate says in Spanish, shaking Miguel from his memory. The passengers remove their life jackets and disembark into ankle deep water on the dock. The mate leads them off the dock and into the shallow water surrounding the brush. There is no dirt or sand for them to make footprints in. Miguel watches as they walk away, saying a short prayer for each of them, and for himself.

The first mate walks beside the group as Oscar leads them out. Oscar is not normally on this part of the trip and he is obviously not happy about being here now. He looks forward and back scolding those who are slow, or those who try to speak to others in the group. As he looks toward the front of the line, a man near the back takes off, running as best he can through the dense brush and shallow water. "Stay with them!" Oscar shouts to the first mate as he goes after the man. The branches and wet earth make it almost impossible to keep up, so he takes out his pistol and shoots repeatedly in the direction of the fleeing man. The man does not stop, running without regard for his body. He is soon out of sight.

Oscar follows the path the man followed hoping to find clues where he went. Instead he finds blood on the leaves, confirming what Oscar thought; he had shot him. *He won't make it*, he thinks. *He will get lost and bleed to death out here, never to be found.*

Up ahead the fleeing man continues to run for quite a while until he is sure no one is in pursuit any longer. He stops to rest a moment, winded but upright. He takes off his wet shirt and for the first time feels the stabbing pain in his back. His shirt is covered in blood and he can feel warm liquid running down his back and into his wet, dirty jeans. He looks down at his stomach and is bleeding from multiple scratches as well, but those were caused by the branches that grabbed his body as he ran through and past them. He reaches around to his back and feels the blood oozing out of a hole in his back. He tears his shirt and ties it tightly around his waist covering the hole to staunch the blood as best he can. He follows the river, occasionally dipping into the water to clean up the bullet wound, but he is weakening with the blood loss. He tries one more time to get to the shoreline and just as he gets there, he falls forward onto a limb overhanging the edge of the river. He raises his head as much as he can, lifts his eyes the rest of the way to the sky. He says a silent prayer and then closes his eyes as the last of his life runs out of his body.

Chapter 13

Magic and I have planned on going back out on her next day off, which is a week away. Since I don't have a full-time day job, I continue the search each day, dragging Scott along when he can make it. Together we are eliminating quite a bit of shoreline over the next five days.

On day one the big Cajun is with me and we run northwest from Manteo toward Point Harbor, the southern point of the mainland that is directly east across the mouth of the Currituck Sound from the Outer Banks towns of Duck and Corolla. I keep the US 158 bridge over the Sound to my starboard and stay to the west of the landmass, passing Powell Point and continuing north up the shoreline of the North River. At Coinjock I cross over to the west shoreline and go a little farther upriver. It just doesn't feel right to me, so I turn back. Heading south now we cover the western shore of the river more quickly.

Day two is the Pasquotank River. Magic and I have already discussed this, and we agree that it is highly unlikely they would be using this river for anything illegal. The Pasquotank takes you up to United States Coast Guard Air Station Elizabeth City and the training facility for the best rescue swimmers in the world. This is where Scott was trained. While we think it unlikely, we agreed that I should run quickly around the shoreline, just in case, so Scott and I do.

Magic and I agreed too that the Perquimans River was just as unlikely if not more so, but on day three and four I run without Scott covering the shoreline and inlets from the Pasquotank up to

the Perquimans. At its entrance I pass the Harvey Point Defense
Testing Facility to the west. This facility was commissioned in
World War II as Naval Air Station Harvey Point, named for the
Harvey family who owned the property since the 1600's and
provided North Carolina with its first native-born governor,
Thomas Harvey. This Department of Defense facility is used today
for various covert training activities and nearby residents are often
treated to the sound of ordinance exploding. There is restricted
airspace around Harvey Point, and there are waters nearby that are
off limits to mariners. I am sure that it possesses highly
sophisticated surveillance technology and I stay far offshore as I
inspect the area. As I said, Magic and I don't think anyone would
be that dumb.

I move on to the west the next day but have no success.
These areas are too populated and open.

Magic and I meet each evening and go over the
locations I have searched that day. Even though she can't go with
me she feels the need to be included in the search and she listens
very closely as I recall the locations and experiences. To be honest,
she is the much smarter of us and I am happy to share what I see
and hear what she has to say about it. She is well-aware of the lack

of progress I have made but remains patient with the process, and with me. I am equally aware that our connection is reaching new levels.

The following Tuesday, Magic is back on *Recovery* resuming the search with me. We start at first light and work all morning covering new shoreline to the west of Harvey Point. We run close to shore, making notes on our map as we eliminate mile after mile. Planes are coming in low over our heads as we pass Northeastern Regional Airport on our way to Edenton, under the US 17 bridge entering the Chowan River.

For the uninitiated, that is Chowan pronounced cho-WAHN, not CHO-win like it looks. Rule of thumb in the Carolinas; always ask how a town name is pronounced. Take Beaufort, for example. Beaufort, North Carolina is down south a little way near Cape Lookout and Morehead City. It is pronounced BOW-firt. Head a bit farther south into South Carolina and you will come to a town also named Beaufort near Charleston. However, this town is pronounced, BUEW-firt. Which is right? Of course, the North Carolina version is, but that's neither here

nor there. To make things even more confusing, there is also a
county in North Carolina named Beaufort, but it does not contain
the town that shares its name; that's in Carteret County. Welcome
to the Carolinas.

We stay toward the east shore passing the communities of
Rockyhock and Arrowhead Beach and into J. Robert Hendrix
Park. It is a hot day again and just after one pm I put Recovery into
neutral and then cut the engine. I don't drop the anchor this time
and we drift sideways slowly up-river as we eat our lunch and drink
our Pepsi.

Magic wants to go for a swim again. Who am I to argue?
She slips out of her jeans, shorts this time. I notice that she is
wearing a different bikini today, the opposite of the one from last
week. The army green bottoms with the white top are just as
appealing and I once again admire her from across the cockpit. I
then giggle at the word "cockpit."

She stands on the gunwale and makes that perfect shallow
dive again, this time surfacing more toward the stern of the boat.
She does a surface dive ten feet away staying under for ten seconds
or so, breaking the water face first just behind the dive platform,

her hair pulling back with the inertia of the water. Instead of her hands smoothing her hair, this time they surface with a white object in them. She places her bikini top on the platform and looks up into my eyes. She definitely knows how to get me.

I look at her, not exactly sure what to say. "You coming?" She asks. *Not yet*, I think, *but give me a minute.* Instead I exclaim, "What the fuck?!" raising my stare from her to the sea pines growing out of the water behind her.

"That's not the response I expected," Magic says.

"Behind you," I say, pointing over her left shoulder toward the shore. She turns her head.

"What the fuck?!" she says, seeing the body of a man dangling on his side three feet above the water, caught in the limbs that extend over the river.

"Exactly," I reply as I toss a towel to the transom. "Get dressed," I say reluctantly, as she pulls herself from the water, wraps herself in the towel and recovers her bikini top from the platform.

We idle up to the overhanging trees and brush as close as I feel comfortable. I run the eye of a line through the center of the midship cleat securing it to both ends, and then run the bitter end around a tree limb and tie it back to the same cleat. We are secured in place by the current.

I notice that I have just enough signal on my phone so I call the Dare County Sheriff's office and tell them about our find. I don't want to use the radio for this information since no channel is truly private. I tell the Sheriff's department our position based upon my GPS, and we are so far up-river that Edenton police and Chowan County Sheriff's office are the responding departments.

While we wait for local authorities to arrive, we inspect the body as best we can without touching or moving him in any way. His face and abdomen are covered in scratches, his torso is wrapped in a dirty tee-shirt that is covered in blood. Our best guess is that the blood is from a wound on his back, although we can't see that from the boat. Even though insects have begun feeding on some of the body, we can tell that he is Hispanic. The similarities to the body we recovered a week ago is impossible to ignore.

"Victim number 2," I say.

"That we know of, yes," Magic responds grimly.

We sit quietly, each in our own thoughts, the heat sapping our energy even though we are under the T-top waiting for the local officers. I give Magic a *Recovery* tee-shirt to replace the shear top she brought with her today, probably more for my jealous benefit than any discomfort on her part. Once they arrive, Magic takes over and gives the responding officers from Edenton PD and Chowan Sheriff's office all the information on how we found him. She then brings them up to speed on the body in Dare County and tells them to contact Doc Watson for more information. They call Dare County Sheriff and it is agreed that the body will be released to Doc Watson for autopsy to speed any connections with our body. The body is bagged and sealed with an evidence clip, and then secured into the coffin box on *Recovery*. No information will be released to the public at this time.

We drop the body off with the Beav who is waiting with the Coroner's van at the boat ramp. We jump into the Whaler and run north in silence, arriving back to *First Draft* after dark. It's been a very long day and we are exhausted. Magic comes inside

92

and we both drop tiredly on the furniture, me in the chair at my desk, Magic on the settee across the salon.

"I don't think we need Doc's autopsy to tell us that this is related to our case," Magic says.

"Nope," I agree. "The question is, what do we do from here?"

"Nothing tonight. I'm too tired," she says.

"And while I am grateful for the lead, I am sorry for the timing," I say.

Magic seems to take a moment to realize what I am talking about. "Oh," she says. "Me too. Maybe another time."

"How about now," I say quietly, but boldly.

"We can't swim naked in the marina, Coop" Magic says with a weak smile, her exhaustion obvious.

"I have a shower with a small tub," I continue. "It's got water." Magic thinks about that for a second.

"Well, we do need to get clean," she says directing her tired eyes so that she is looking directly into mine. I can see by her expression when she decides. She slowly stands up and walks closer to where I still sit. She peels off the Recovery tee shirt and slowly reaches behind her, untying the back of her bikini top, slipping it over her head and letting it fall to the floor. She then unbuttons her jean shorts sliding them down to her ankles before stepping out of them one foot at a time leaving on only her bikini bottom. Now standing mostly naked above me, she extends her hand out in front of her and says, "Lead the way Captain." I decide in this moment that she can call me 'Captain' any time she likes.

I stand as I take her hand and begin to guide her toward the stern of the boat and the master stateroom. "Maybe we should get a little dirty first," she whispers as she wraps her arms around my arm pressing her breasts against my skin.

"As you wish," I say. And by the low, understanding moan I hear from her, I know I said it out loud.

Chapter 14

Miguel is sitting in a folding chair across a card table from Oscar in the same detached garage where he watched the murder of his friend Hector. He wonders if the chair he sits in now is the same one his friend died in. The garage is on a large plot of land just outside of Gatesville, North Carolina just thirty miles north of Edenton, and even closer to Murfreesboro across the Chowan River to the west.

The garage is orderly, but not clean. It's sparse furnishings include four folding chairs and an old dining room table made of pine, scratched over time with indentations from writing utensils, perhaps the marks of children doing homework when its life included such happy things. There is no air conditioning and Miguel looks into the spinning blades of the portable fan in the corner, its motion and hum pulling him in, his thoughts wandering. He runs his finger across a mark in the table that looks like a plus sign.

"I can't do this!" Angela exclaims, placing her head in her left hand, slamming the pencil onto the table with the other, with a frustrated scowl on her face. Miguel is sitting to her right looking down at the math problem partially solved on the piece of paper in front her. He looks at his daughter, her dark hair covering the left side of her face, her eyes squinting, her teeth clenched behind pursed, angry lips. He holds back a giggle.

"Yes, you can Angel," he says softly as he places his hand atop hers, the pencil underneath. "Look at me." Angela continues

to look down at the table, focusing on the marks in the wood and not the math problem. Miguel applies more pressure on her hand, a compassionate touch gently squeezing her fingers. She looks up meeting his gaze.

Looking back down at the paper, Miguel slides the pencil out from under Angela's hand, points the lead at the first column. "Add down the farthest right column, what do you get," he says looking at a nine and a five and handing her the pencil.

"Nine plus five is fourteen, right?" she answers, putting a four at the bottom of the farthest right column.

"Right, angel. Now carry the one over to the next column and add those together." The eight and one of eighty-nine and fifteen are next.

"Eight plus one is nine, plus the other one is ten," she says writing the ten to the left of the four.

"So, what is eighty-nine plus fifteen?" he asks patiently.

"One hundred and four?"

"Are you asking me, or telling me?" Miguel says with a smile.

"Telling you, Daddy," she says, not adding the "Like, duh!" that her tone implies.

"Very good, angel. See, you can do it," Miguel says taking his daughters hand in his again. "You can do anything you put your mind to Angela."

Miguel is looking down at the table, his finger tracing a memory. He sees Angela smile bright in his mind, a sad grin on his own face.

Jefe promised that after ten trips, Miguel's debt would be paid, and he would be reunited with his daughter. The trip they are planning is his tenth and final trip, although this has not come up in any of the planning discussions. Miguel worries that broaching the subject will anger Jefe.

He wants to see his sweet angel. No, he needs to see her. He needs to know that she is okay. He needs to hold her and tell her how proud he is of her; how much he loves her. "You can do anything you put your mind to angel," he says under his breath.

"Thursday evening we will head out and pick up our next shipment," Jefe says, pointing to a location on a map laying on the table.

Shipment, Miguel thinks to himself. That is what these people are to him. They are cargo, inventory to make money from. He is disgusted and he can't help but let out a frustrated sigh.

"You have a problem amigo?" Jefe asks.

"No. No problem Jefe. I am missing my daughter and want to see her," Miguel responds truthfully.

"I told you, finish these trips and your debt will be repaid. I brought you to this country amigo, you can be a bit more appreciative," Jefe says. "When you have done this, I will bring your sweet Angela to you."

Hearing Jefe use his daughters name, Miguel feels physically ill. He hides it by putting a hand to his mouth and feigning a cough. "This is the last trip, true Jefe?" he says, a little vomit making its way up his throat and almost into his mouth.

"What's wrong Miguel? You don't trust me?"

Not at all, Miguel thinks. "Completely," he says instead. Jefe grins at Miguel. It's a grin that has not a shred of happiness in it. It is a grin of satisfaction that comes from controlling another individual's life, a grin that belongs on a devil.

Jefe lays out the plan for next Thursday keeping an eye on Miguel.

Chapter 15

Magic receives the Sheriff's office permission to include me as an official part of the investigation. This means that I will be paid a daily consulting rate for my time, and expenses for the use of my boat, similar to the arrangement we have for recovering bodies. I am still not a cop, but I am probably as close as I will ever get. I see myself as Gibbs on *NCIS*; Gibbs in the early episodes, not the one's today. I am a young Gibbs. In a rare moment of insecurity, I hope I am not Barnie Fife.

Over the next week, as an official team, Magic and I continue our search up-river, focusing on areas within a short boat ride from where we found our latest body. We are using *Recovery* and not the Sheriff's boat because we are well outside of Dare County's jurisdiction. This, and the fact that Magic wears a bikini each day as part of our "cover," allows us to interject some distraction during our breaks. We finally get our naked swim during one of our lunches that was ruined by a rainstorm. We made the most of it discarding wet bathing suits on the deck and jumping into the warm water.

"You know this can't last, right?" Magic says to me as we float near the boat, her legs wrapped around my waist, arms around my neck, me treading water for both of us.

"Is that okay if it doesn't?" I ask.

"I don't know," she says moving her face closer to mine, her eyes piercing me, and then moving her mouth close to my ear as she pulls me closer. "I don't want this to end."

"I don't either," I say into her ear, exhaling onto her neck as she scratches the fingers of her left hand up my back.

"So, what do we do?" she asks.

"I have no answer for that. You are the smarter one, you tell me," I say, instead of *stay with me and we can make a great life!* as I am thinking.

"Let's solve this thing and then we should sit down and talk," she says, her mouth on my neck. Magic pauses a moment pressing her cheek into my shoulder, the sound of water under the hull like a small horse walking slowly nearby. She leans back, her hands behind my neck holding her face at arm's length from mine. She looks deeply at me again. "Is that okay?" she asks.

"Of course," I say, knowing it is the best I am going to get today. Also knowing that her plan is our best course of action. "Does that talk include being naked?" I say with a smile, lightening the mood.

She smiles and kisses me a long, wet kiss that I accept eagerly. Pulling back she says, "Perhaps."

I'll take it.

After our swim and a little more activity on the coffin box of *Recovery* – don't judge me – we begin to move again, searching the shoreline. We are trying to find a place a boat could dock. This might be a true dock, but if so, it would be very secluded. More likely it is a structure, manmade or natural, that allows a boat to get close to shore and disembark passengers. Magic and I are both skilled Captains and we know that we could put a boat against any number of different structures that would serve as a dock in need. We search for those as well.

"There!" Magic exclaims from the bow of the Guardian pointing off the starboard bow. I look in the direction she is pointing and see a railroad tie that seems to be suspended between the roots of the pine sea brush surrounding it. "How is your depth?" she asks.

"Plenty of water, staying steady at nine feet."

Magic looks back at me and says, "Idle up slowly and watch your depth, see if you can get in there."

"In where?" I say as only a prepubescent teen can.

Sensing the innuendo Magic chooses the high road, "In the creek to the railroad tie," she says. Waiting a beat for best comedic affect, she adds "Butthead."

"Aye aye, Captain."

We idle slowly toward the railroad tie. The depth barely changes at all staying at almost nine feet the entire way. As we get to within a couple yards the depth begins to get shallower, but only slightly. There is still plenty of water for vessels larger than *Recovery*.

"You're clear to dock if depth is still good," Magic says.

I cut the wheel hard to port and slide slowly into the railroad tie resting starboard side in. Magic grabs the tie with her hands holding us off the 'dock' and keeping us still. The water is barely moving and there is no need for us to tie off to anything.

As the boat comes to rest, I notice decking just past the railroad tie. It is under water so not visible from the river, nor from the sky on most days I am sure. "Sonofabitch," I say in a hushed voice.

"This is it," Magic says. "This is where they dock. Who knows how many people have had to disembark here and walk through the water and brush." She looks down the rough path leading inland. I can see her putting the pieces together in her mind. I start to see it too.

"You think they are human smugglers delivering people through here?" I say. "This seems a long distance from where that is a problem," I add thinking of the border communities in California and Texas, and the coastlines of Florida and all along the Gulf of Mexico."

"That's what makes it so perfect," Magic says, never taking her eyes off the dock and the rudimentary trail that leads inland. "If you want to sneak a keg into a dorm you don't come through the front door," she says using a metaphor she knows I will understand. "This is it," she confidently adds.

"What is it?" I ask so that I can hear aloud what she is thinking.

"This is where they started their run, the two men we have in autopsy in Manteo. This is where they were first hunted." She pauses and then continues, "and they both died close to here." Magic pauses. "I wonder how many more we are missing," she says more solemnly.

"And what do we do now?" I ask. Magic looks at me for a moment and then reaches into her backpack for a notebook and her phone.

"Mark this location in your GPS and let's go," she says. I do as I am told.

I am completely impressed as I watch Magic work, formulating a plan as we motor back upriver. She places a call first to Edenton PD, and then to Chowan Sheriff's office, informing them both of our findings. She schedules a conference call to begin in thirty minutes with both departments, including the Dare County Sheriff's Office as well. During the break before the call we motor faster toward Manteo as Magic writes down the plan of action she will share.

Exactly 30 minutes later we are idling as all parties join the call. Magic is the lead here and she instructs everyone on the surveillance schedule we will follow. She and I are one team that will take an eight-hour shift each day, Edenton PD and Chowan Sheriff taking the other two. The surveillance area is too far outside of Dare County's jurisdiction to commit any more resources to the stake out. I am going to be part of a stake out. I can hear the *Law & Order* tones in my head.

I am looking at Magic in admiration. It is oddly fulfilling watching her put together a plan of execution and then communicate it to a team without the least bit of self-doubt. She is in command and she embraces it. All three offices listen and verbally agree when Magic pauses for them to do so. It may sound strange, but I feel proud of her.

After the plan is confirmed and all parties have said their 'Goodbyes,' Magic presses the red button on the screen of her smartphone to end the call. She asks, "You good with that?"

"As you wish," I say, channeling my best Wesley. I am looking at her adoringly and she smiles and looks away. I steal a glance at her boobs. I am still a guy after all.

Chapter 16

Miguel has just completed what he hopes is his last pickup. He still needs to take his passengers back to the dock and drop them off, but then his agreement with Oscar is over. His heart breaks with every life he brings to the shores of North Carolina, every life that is changed for the worse because of who *he* first trusted. He knows he needs to make it work though, and he hopes each passenger will see the goodness in his eyes. He wishes he could tell each about his Angela, about how she is being held someplace, he doesn't know where. He is a father first, and everything else is a distant second or farther down the list of importance. He is a *good man*, he tells himself, and under his forced circumstance he strives to do something good for each of them, to make their lives better, if even just for a moment.

The decision Miguel made to save the boat the night he and Angela were to land in North Carolina has put him here in this place, right now. It has put Angela in a location only Jefe and God know, and lead to the deaths of his friends José and Hector. Should he have done something differently? Should he have let the boat drift and run aground, perhaps even sink, killing all aboard?

No, he knows he would do the same thing again if he were to relive it. He is a trained boat Captain and keeping passengers safe is part of his DNA. His mistake was trusting Jefe in the first place, but even that decision he can't second-guess because he simply didn't have the information he has now.

Because Miguel knows what they are going through, and what is ahead, he works hard to make his passengers as comfortable as possible. He personally hands each a life jacket and a bottle of

water, and gives them a gentle smile and a nod as a silent,
'*Welcome aboard.*' He knows though, the disappointment they are
feeling. He came over the same way and while his path changed
upon arrival, he has witnessed this scene again and again. They
think they have paid for passage to the United States and to a better
life, and ultimately, they have. Before that part of their lives can
begin though, they will go through hell first. It is becoming clear
that they have made a deal with the devil, and that 'freedom and
opportunity' will have to wait.

When Miguel first met Jefe, he saw a successful man. He
was dressed well, wore nice jewelry and stood tall in boots that cost
three-months or more of Miguel's salary. Jefe talked about how he
would deliver Miguel's family to the United States and what riches
awaited them. As most Mexican's, Miguel had a family member
already living in the States. Jefe's role, as he described it, was to
connect family with family, and for that service each surrendered
savings they had struggled months to compile, many times years.
Regardless of the cost, the opportunity of life in the US was worth
the investment.

Hurting inside, Miguel steers his vessel through Oregon
Inlet in relatively calm seas. A storm is following them in from the

east. The calm before the storm is real and the east wind is pushing
them inland.

Miguel captains his ship through the inlet, east of Wanchese
and Manteo, up past Kill Devil Hills on the barrier island to the
east, and then turns west up the Albemarle Sound. Lightning is off
his stern and by the smell he knows the rain will catch them soon.
He keeps the throttles at the same speed, doing nothing different
than he has done on each of his last nine trips. He wants to get to
the dock and be done with this, forever. The sea was once a love
of his life, but now he wonders if he will ever be able to find its joy
again. He wants to see his Angela, to hold her and tell her how
much Daddy loves her, and how sorry he is for not being there for
her for the past six months. He dreads hearing the stories of what
she has endured, but he also wants to hear her voice as he holds her
in his arms.

Miguel idles up to the dock just as the rain catches them.
As he always does, he looks to his stern before slowing even though
there has never once been another vessel behind him at this point
of the journey. Out of the corner of his eye he thinks he sees a glint
of light up-river a couple hundred yards and close to the eastern
shore. The rain starts to fall harder as Miguel reverses the port

engine, the Blackfin rotating on its center and exposing its starboard side to the shoreline. As the boat settles completely broadside to its target, Miguel puts the starboard engine into reverse for just a couple seconds, and then both engines into neutral allowing the vessel to gently rest against the railroad tie.

He looks up into the arriving storm. He can see that there is something different about the waterline behind him and looks more intently. Lightning brightens the night and he sees the outline of an approaching center console silhouetted against the horizon.

Chapter 17

It is dark and Magic and I are in *Recovery* on our third surveillance shift in three days. On the previous two nights we didn't have any activity at all. Let me rephrase; we didn't have any activity that had anything to do with our surveillance mission. We did engage in some on-vessel activities, however. The Sheriff's Department and Edenton PD who had earlier shifts had witnessed no activity related to the mission either. I can't speak to their on-boat activities.

We are moving slowly up-river, navigation lights off, "Running dark."

"What?" Magic says. I haven't stopped vocalizing my thoughts, I guess.

"Nothing," I reply.

"Yeah, right!" Magic replies with a smile, looking back over her shoulder at me. She is getting to know me, I guess. Her face changes and she looks up into the air putting an ear to the wind.

"Shh…," she says.

"What do you hear…"

"Shhh!" Magic cuts me off.

I hear it before I see it, the rumble of a boat coming up the river. I can just make out the silhouette of a vessel against the sky behind it, a small Sportfish about a quarter mile southeast of us. We are still camouflaged against the pine brush shoreline; there is no way they can see the outline of *Recovery* without the aid of the moon or an electric light. The boat idles past us in the dark heading in the direction of the railroad tie. We begin to follow at a distance.

The vessel continues up-river and then turns into the tributary toward the dock. Its lights are off and that alone makes the boat suspicious. I take care that from their view the shoreline is behind us and they will not make out our straight lines among the tangled branches. I am counting on the sound of their own engines cloaking the low boil of my 4-stroke outboards. The Hondas are whisper quiet at this speed and we stealthily run behind the fishing vessel as the rain increases.

I have a T-top with no enclosure on the Guardian so windblown rain begins to pelt our faces and bodies. "Where is your rain gear?" Magic asks me quietly.

"In the console below you," I whisper back.

Magic removes the hatch cover and takes two sets of rain gear out placing one on the helm seat next to me. She gears up and looks at mine, noticing it is still sitting in the same place.

"Aren't you going to put on your rain gear?" Magic says, says using more breath than voice.

"No," I respond in a hushed tone as well. "I learned from a charter Captain years ago on a photo shoot in the Florida Keys that the human body is waterproof. He was a tough ex-Marine with a tattoo on his forearm and since then I haven't bothered with rain gear."

"First of all," Magic begins still using her surveillance voice, "Once a Marine, always a Marine. Retired, not ex," she corrects pausing for effect. "And second, I don't see 'Semper Fi' on you!" she says extending her arm with a rain jacket toward me. I put it on, but I ignore the pants. It's a small protest and Magic lets me win that much.

I settle *Recovery* directly in the wake of the fishing boat now, following at the same speed. It is dark and the foam in the water and the sound of the vessel's engine is about all I have for navigation. The wind is increasing, and rain begins to slam into the windscreen that both Magic and I are now crouched behind. The good thing is that there is no way they can hear us in these conditions.

The fishing vessel continues up the small tributary and idles toward the shoreline in the direction of the railroad tie. There looks to be nothing that the boat is going to dock against, but we know exactly where they are going. This is where their trip ends.

"Call the Sheriff," I tell Magic. I look back and see that she is already on the phone and giving our location. She is always a step ahead of me. She hangs up the phone and says, "They are on their way but with the weather, it's going to take them just a little bit of time."

By the sound of the engines I can tell that the Captain has begun maneuvers to dock the boat. I can hear one of the transmissions shift into reverse, the rain beginning to fall harder, pelting the Whaler. It is getting more difficult to see the fishing vessel and beginning to obscure the already faint view that we have of it.

"We need to make decisions now, Magic," I say.

Magic looks from the sportfish, down the shoreline and back behind us. She is calculating risk; the risk of losing the suspects, the risk of us losing our lives. She is the one in charge here and we both know it. Any decision has to be hers. For once I say nothing.

A bright lightning flash reveals the Captain on the flybridge looking directly back at us as his vessel slides starboard side into the railroad tie.   Magic doesn't hesitate. "Go!" she says emphatically. "Go now!" pointing toward the sportfish.

I slam onto the throttles pushing them to the stops and *Recovery* responds immediately. The bow raises and quickly planes off, hurtling toward our prey at thirty-five knots in a pouring rainstorm in the dark.

Chapter 18

Miguel cuts the engines as he looks aft. He hears the center console now and knows this is the last time, one way or another. He feels some relief along with fear, but overall, he is calm, almost content with allowing the universe to make decisions for him now. Content that it isn't Jefe calling the shots anymore. He takes the keys out of each of the ignitions and drops them to the floor of the flybridge, and then kicks them aft allowing them to slide off the top of the ladder and fall into the cockpit below. He looks up into the rain, letting it cleanse him. He can taste his sweat as the water runs off his face and into his mouth. He is crying, hoping that God will cleanse his sins too.

With the Blackfin's motors silent now, the first mate hears the approaching vessel. He turns immediately toward the sound raising the AK-47 he has been carrying for the past five miles. He investigates the dark night for the direction of the sound. He makes no attempt to identify the incoming boat and begins firing on full-automatic into the darkness, the approaching engine sound his only site. He is spraying ammunition wildly into the night, but he knows that he has the advantage. This particular weapon doesn't require much skill to hit a target; it just takes ammunition and time. He fires keeping the barrel of the rifle at sea level, moving it side-to-side.

Chapter 19

There are bright flashes coming from the stern of the boat and the unmistakable sound of automatic gunfire; unmistakable to me only because I have heard it on television. I know the weather and distance is in our favor, but I also know that even a spasmatic blind man can hit a target with a fully automatic weapon. It scares the shit out of me.

I spin the wheel to port away from shore and the gunfire, turning *Recovery* around and increasing the distance between our two vessels. Bullets are hitting the water around us and some are hitting the Guardian as well. Magic jumps into action and instinctively crouches below the gunwale and begins shooting in the direction of the gunfire. For the first time since I read the original brochure, I think about the hull of a Boston Whaler Guardian and its promise to hold off up to one thousand rounds. Rounds are hitting the hull and sure enough, none are coming through into the cockpit.

"Go toward them!" Magic yells over the sound of the engines, the increasing wind and the rain. I turn the boat to port again without reducing the throttles. The Whaler leans in carving a sharp curve into the water, turning us around and accelerating back toward the fishing vessel. I am leaning to starboard looking around the right side of the windshield as rain slams into the hard plastic.

Magic continues to fire into the dark toward the flashes of light that are continuous now from the shoreline in front of us. Rain is pouring down, lightning coming in from the east as thunder rolls over the sea. I look up at Magic crouched down behind the gunwale and am in awe. I know she is trained, but to see her so focused in a true life or death situation, I am impressed. I wonder what she sees in me. She can have anyone she wants and yet she chooses me. I am proud as I watch her; proud of her bravery, proud of the man she sees in me.

I feel warm liquid flowing down my right shoulder before I feel the sting in my neck. My right hand still on the throttles, I take my left hand off the wheel reaching over to cover where the stinging is coming from, just below my right ear. I feel liquid running between my fingers, but it isn't water. It is thicker and much warmer than the cool rain. I quickly realize that it is my own blood. I am not sure what to do so I do nothing but run the boat and try to slow my blood loss.

I am looking forward as we approach the fishing vessel and beginning to get sleepy. The flashes of light in front of me begin to look mystical, like blinking stars bouncing off a sea decorated with thousands of raindrop-sized fountains. There are loud bangs too, drums that seem to be in cadence with the lightshow I am experiencing. Then there are blue lights to my left, passing by and moving away to join the show in front of me.

I can still feel forward movement and the lights seem to be coming closer and closer. It is beautiful. I see a shape in front of me stand and turn in my direction. I hear Magic's voice and for the first time there is fear in it. That worries me. "Slow down Coop!" she screams as she steps toward me.

Even as I feel myself fading, I obey her. I can't move my right arm, so I take my left hand from my neck and find the throttle. It is strangely slippery as I grab it and I wonder what I have spilled on it. I grip it as tight as I can and feel a viscous liquid squeeze out between my fingers as I pull the throttles back. The boat begins to slow, and I hear a 'click' as the throttles fall into neutral. My body continues forward as the Whaler comes to a stop. My legs are weakening, and I slide down the helm, my face hitting the wheel as I crumble to the deck. My body stops moving only because I hit the floor in front of the helm, laying on my right side, my face looking forward.

Magic reaches me as I hit the deck. Her right arm is pointing at something in front of us and flashes keep coming from the tips of her finger. She turns toward me dropping to the floor next to me and grabbing my neck, applying pressure for some reason.

"Stay with me Coop!" I hear her say. "Stay with me!"

I can see her face and I am confused. Her gaze is one of dread and I wonder why she fears me. "Stay with me Coop!" she says again.

I want to ease her fear and attempt a smile. It is weak at best, I know. "As you wish," I rasp through failing breath before succumbing to complete darkness.

Chapter 20

Miguel says a quick prayer and then looks down into the cockpit from the flybridge helm. He sees the deckhand lift his weapon and begin firing wildly at the dark silhouette of a medium-sized center console approaching from down river. He can now tell that the vessel looks a lot like a police or military boat, and he feels some relief. *It all ends today*, he thinks. Any sense of relief is not shared by his passengers or crew. He is sure the passengers are cowering below-deck trying to stay safe, digging themselves deeper and deeper into the cabin. His crewman has his finger pressed down on the trigger, the uninterrupted gunfire delivering deadly projectiles in the direction of the incoming vessel. Avoiding the gunfire, the center console begins to turn around and is then moving from the danger. Miguel's heart sinks.

"Vamanos! Vamanos!" the deckhand yells up at Miguel, pausing his assault. He is animatedly pointing back the way they came, into the oncoming storm, rain pelting the deck around him. Miguel simply stares at the man. He has had enough. It's over. He is done.

"Vamanos!" the man screams once again, lightning flashing across his rain-soaked face revealing angry and scared eyes. He sees the keys on the deck below him. He bends down. picks them up and throws them up at Miguel. He reaches his right hand behind his back freeing the pistol that rests there and points it up at Miguel. "Ahora!" he yells, his voice clear through the sound of the pelting rain. "Now!" he says again in English for emphasis.

Out of the corner of his right eye Miguel can see that the center console has turned around and is approaching once more.

This time there is a flash coming from the incoming boat, each followed almost immediately by a "bang!" It is gunfire, this time in his direction. Behind the center console are blue lights of more than one police boat speeding toward them. Men who have been waiting in the shallow water hiding in the brush in the rain lift their weapons and begin to fire in the direction of the incoming vessels.

"No," Miguel says, his voice getting lost in the increasing wind, rain and gunfire.

"Vamanos!" the deckhand screams once more, shaking the pistol at Miguel. Bullets are flying in both directions now, outgoing low from the brush to his right, incoming all around him, but lower. Blue lights are almost here now.

"No!" he says loudly through the cacophony of sound including automatic weapon fire, pistol gunshots, high-revving outboard motors from smaller boats and the rumbling inboard power from police cutters. "No," he says again more quietly, more to himself now.

The flash and the bang from the pistol below him are in synch. He feels a punch under his ribcage and is propelled back into the helm seat which is turned around. He slouches in the seat pushing himself up with his right leg as much as his strength will allow. He reaches into his right breast pocket and takes out a picture. He stares into the eyes of his daughter as his life begins to slip away.

The gunfire is over now, and Magic has left Coop in the capable hands of paramedics who accompanied the Sheriff's department. She is standing in the cockpit of the fishing vessel looking down at a deckhand, an AK strapped around his body, a bullet hole in the center of his head, blood on the deck running out the drain holes at the stern. The site of blood in a fishing vessel is nothing new. Today though, it is human blood and her heart sinks a little. Training or not, people have died here today.

She climbs the ladder to the flybridge and sees the Captain sitting there holding something in his hands. Unable to identify the item, Magic pulls her weapon pointing it at the Captain, lighting him up with the flashlight she is holding in her left hand under the barrel as she has been taught. Immediately she knows he is not a threat and holsters her weapon.

She reaches the man checking his breathing and pulse. Both are weak. He is dying. She looks down into his hand and notices that what he is holding is a picture. As she tries to remove it from his hand the man grips it and lifts his head looking straight at her.

"Find her," he says raggedly, his breathing barely strong enough to get the words out. "Por favor... por favor," he says, his head slumping forward, his hand releasing his grip on the picture. She holds onto it and looks down into eyes that are exactly the same as the man in front of her. Magic applies pressure to his wound as she yells, "Medic!"

Bringing her attention back to the Captain she says, "Lo prometo," quietly into his ear. Pulling her head back she looks down at the young girl in the photo. "I promise," she says.

Epilogue

I wake looking up into ceiling tiles and fluorescent lights, a cadence of beeps in succession are coming from somewhere just behind me to my right. If this was a movie I would say, "Where am I?" Having seen a lot of movies and television shows where this has happened, I immediately know I am in a hospital bed. I am also familiar with this 'waking up in a hospital' thing; *at least this time it wasn't due to my drinking*, I say to myself as if getting shot is a better alternative. To me, at this moment, I guess it is.

I look to my left and see Magic sitting there. She is holding my hand, asleep in a chair next to my bed with a copy of *Vigilant Charity*, the most recent volume of her favorite sea adventure series laying open across her chest.

"Good morning," I rasp as I weakly squeeze her hand. Magic stirs, rubs her eyes and looks at me.

"Good evening to you," she says with a tired smile standing up and looking down at me. "You've been resting for a couple days."

This also happens in the movies and on television, but I am still surprised. I am also upset that I missed the plot twist considering this, also, has happened to me before. She informs me that I have been in a medically induced coma for two days. I smile up at her, or at least I think I do. She is beautiful. She has always been beautiful. But after sleeping in a hospital chair for two days and backlit by the harshest light known to man, she is still stunning. Now that is beautiful.

"It's good to have you back," she says brushing my hair back with her hand and kissing me gently on the cheek. My memory of the event stops at the point of running *Recovery* toward the fishing boat, so Magic fills me in.

As the rain was starting to pick up and we came under fire, Edenton PD boats were arriving on scene. Magic let the local cops take over the fight and came to help me, my body on the floor behind the protection of the Guardian gunwale. She took over the wheel and closed the distance between the *Recovery* and the fishing boat as the fight was slowing.

Edenton PD was just ahead and firing at the stern of the fishing boat from two other vessels. Two other gunmen were firing from the shore and one of the other police boats quickly eliminated that threat.

As the guy on the stern of the fishing boat ran out of ammo in his AK, Magic and Edenton Police closed quickly, Magic arriving first. As Magic moved to the bow of the Guardian and peered into the cockpit, the man on the deck lifted his right hand holding a pistol. Magic knew there was no time for her to defend herself or even to jump into the water as escape. She was done.

A loud 'crack' to her left and the threat was eliminated, the bullet from the officer's Glock striking the man between the eyes, taking his life, and saving Magic's. There was no other defense from the fishing boat.

Paramedics had me so Magic headed onto the fishing vessel. Going up the ladder to the upper helm she found the Captain slouched, bleeding and dying at the wheel. She tells me about the picture in his hand and his words to her. "Find her." Looking into her eyes I know she has already made the decision to do exactly that.

Over the past two days, while I slept, authorities found that the Captain's name was Miguel Cortez. He is from a fishing town in Mexico and was brought to the US, along with his daughter, by a Coyote, a human smuggler. Upon reaching the US the Coyote needed Miguel's skill as a boat captain and used his daughter as leverage to get him to work for him. She shows me her picture telling me that her name is Angela and she is still missing. There is something familiar about the little girl, but I can't put my finger on it. She then shows me a picture of Miguel.

I see the same eyes I had just seen in the picture of the little girl. I recognize him immediately from lunch at the diner. I clearly see in my mind the three men sitting at the table in the corner and realize that I have information the police probably do not have yet.

Magic mistakes my alarm as anxiety and starts to soothe me with her words and touch. "I'm sorry Coop," she says. "I can tell you the rest of this later. You get some sleep."

"No," I say, strength coming back to me now. "I know this guy."

"What?" she says.

"I was at Duke's a few weeks ago after we found the body of the first Mexican guy. This man was at a table in the corner with two others."

"Wait," Magic says, holding a finger up and stepping out into the hallway grabbing a police officer who has been stationed outside my door. "Continue," she says as the officer pulls out a small notebook and a pen.

"Why is there a police officer outside my door?" I ask first.

"Coop," Magic replies. "We can get into that later. Tell us about this man and the other two."

So, I do. I tell them about how the nicely dressed guy didn't seem very kind to the other two men. I give descriptions of the other two and there is a look of recognition in Magic and the Officer's eyes.

"What?" I ask. The officer answers this time.

"The men who were captured and killed during the fight that night were just workers. They were moving immigrants into the US illegally, but they are not the leader. The guy you saw, is," he says.

"Many talked about 'Jefe,' but none were able to give a description or a name," Magic continues. "He was not captured."

I am feeling a bit weaker now but am taking some pride that I have been able to contribute something to the investigation. Magic senses my slipping attention, thanks the officer and walks him to the door before returning to my bedside. She looks down at me again, her police persona left behind at the door. "How are you feeling?" she asks.

"Like I got shot."

She laughs and smiles just a little bit, rubbing my arm, tears forming in her eyes. "What are we going to do with you?" she says.

"I have some ideas," I offer weakly.

"I bet you do," she says, laughing more this time and standing upright next to my bed. Magic takes her right hand and runs her fingers through her hair revealing her face in the way women do. I feel a stir. That gets me every time.

THE END

Acknowledgements

Almost twenty-five years ago I wrote a short story that I hoped to someday publish as a novel. My life took me into the media and advertising businesses and writing for others, which meant getting paid actual money for my work. My life also included a growing family that required not just money, but my attention too.

I set aside that work until five years ago. I embarked on a renewed path moving my life from south Florida back to North Carolina where I went to college, where my own family first began, and where my high school-aged daughters now lived with their mother. I was ending one chapter of my life and beginning a new one.

I dusted off the old story and began the work of expanding it into a novel. The problem was that the story was almost twenty-five years old and a lot had changed in that time. My main character was a college-aged version of myself, and technology improvements had made my once timely story a period piece. Visionaries had changed how we communicate and connect, and I had grown older. And Amazon had dramatically changed the publishing business.

I have always been an avid reader and about that same time I discovered through Amazon recommendations a writer named Ed Robinson, and a genre best known as *Sea Adventure*. His *Breeze* books took me deeper into the genre with authors like Wayne Stinnett, Michael Reisig and Dawn Lee McKenna. These authors' recommendations helped me find Rodney Riesel, Kimberli A. Bindschatel, Cap Daniels and more. My literary world had brightened into stories that included beautiful sunrises, the elusive green flash, sometimes violent storms at sea and of course interesting characters connecting in more intimate ways. My story was sepia toned at best.

I wrote something new, a single paragraph about a recovering alcoholic who's job it was to recover dead bodies from the sea for a stretched-too-thin Sheriff's office. I set it aside.

Two years ago, on vacation in Oak Island North Carolina the group I was with wanted to go to the beach for the day. I am not a "lay on the beach" kind of person so I brought a chair, umbrella and my notebook; and the dusty paragraph I had set aside. I proceeded to move my chair about 100 yards down the beach away from everyone and outlined the story of Grayson Cooper and Zaina Majik that lead to this work.

Thank you first to those friends who I very rudely ignored for the better part of a five-hour beach day. Star, Cynthia, Sandra, Charles and my Sarah, this book is why I drank your beer and only waved in your direction from time to time.

Thank you also to my early readers: Michael Doolittle, Captain Matthew "Hoop" Hooper, John Cooper and Rickie Castaneda. No matter how defensive I may seem, your input is always appreciated!

Thank you to all the authors I mentioned earlier. Each of you has inspired me in your own way to take this *leap of faith* (nod to Ed). Special thanks to Wayne Stinnett whose wealth of knowledge on self-publishing he openly shares through his blog for aspiring authors, and who quickly responds to website messages and emails from an unknown. If you haven't read

Wayne – and if you read my book I can't believe that you haven't – you can find out more at www.WayneStinnett.com.

Finally, thank you to my love Sarah and my daughters Kira and Ella. The grace and strength in each of you is a guide I use when I write female characters. Fun, smart, and sometimes a sarcastic wiseass, I hope you see some of you in Zaina Majik.

Doug Brisotti
November 2019

About the Author

Doug Brisotti splits his time living on land in Greensboro North Carolina and on a boat in Beaufort (NC). He grew up on the water on Long Island, first in Glen Cove and then in Bay Shore, spending family vacations on Peconic Bay in Mattituck. After Guilford College and ten more years

Photo Credit: Ella Brisotti

in North Carolina, Doug spent fifteen years in south Florida before moving back to Greensboro to be close to his daughters.

Doug is a licensed Captain and runs charters out of Beaufort (www.NextChapterCharters.com). More likely he can be found in his 17' Boston Whaler Montauk, *storyteller,* hanging out on a sandbar or having a drink with friends at a local watering hole.

Doug works for Curtis Media Group in Raleigh. He has two college-aged daughters, Kira and Ella, and lives with his "crew," his love Sarah and their ani-mates Lyla (dog) and Nahla (cat).

Previous Work

Non-Fiction

I'ms Okay, 2017, available on Amazon.com

Made in the USA
Monee, IL
13 February 2023

27695642R00090